"I can't get you out of my mind—"

"I know what you're up to."

"I doubt that." Hayes leaned toward her, his hand looping around the back of McKenzie's neck as he gently drew her to him. "Because if you could see what I was up to, then you'd know I was about to kiss you."

He brushed his lips over hers, then pulled back to gaze into her eyes. "Sorry, I couldn't resist."

"You don't have to treat me as if I'm made out of glass and might break," she said. "I'm a lot stronger than I look."

"Is that right?" He looped an arm around her waist and pulled her to him right there in the street between their vehicles. Her full lips parted in surprise. Her sweet, warm breath comingled with his own. She let out a soft moan as he tasted her. Drawing her even closer, he deepened the kiss, demanding more.

RESCUE AT CARDWELL RANCH

***New York Times* Bestselling Author**

B.J. DANIELS

Recycling programs for this product may not exist in your area.

This one is for David Rummel,
who makes me laugh with his stories and
his wonderful joy for life. You definitely
make our lives more fun.

ISBN-13: 978-0-373-69764-9

RESCUE AT CARDWELL RANCH

This edition published by arrangement with Harlequin Books S.A.

For questions and comments about the quality of this book, please contact us at CustomerService@Harlequin.com.

Printed in U.S.A.

ABOUT THE AUTHOR

New York Times bestselling author B.J. Daniels wrote her first book after a career as an award-winning newspaper journalist and author of thirty-seven published short stories. That first book, *Odd Man Out,* received a four-and-a-half-star review from *RT Book Reviews* and went on to be nominated for Best Intrigue that year. Since then, she has won numerous awards, including a career achievement award for romantic suspense and many nominations and awards for best book.

Daniels lives in Montana with her husband, Parker, and two springer spaniels, Spot and Jem. When she isn't writing, she snowboards, camps, boats and plays tennis. Daniels is a member of Mystery Writers of America, Sisters in Crime, International Thriller Writers, Kiss of Death and Romance Writers of America.

To contact her, write to B.J. Daniels, P.O. Box 1173, Malta, MT 59538, or email her at bjdaniels@mtintouch.net. Check out her website, www.bjdaniels.com.

Books by B.J. Daniels

HARLEQUIN INTRIGUE

897—CRIME SCENE AT CARDWELL RANCH
996—SECRET OF DEADMAN'S COULEE*
1002—THE NEW DEPUTY IN TOWN*
1024—THE MYSTERY MAN OF WHITEHORSE*
1030—CLASSIFIED CHRISTMAS*
1053—MATCHMAKING WITH A MISSION*
1059—SECOND CHANCE COWBOY*
1083—MONTANA ROYALTY*
1125—SHOTGUN BRIDE§
1131—HUNTING DOWN THE HORSEMAN§
1137—BIG SKY DYNASTY§
1155—SMOKIN' SIX-SHOOTER§
1161—ONE HOT FORTY-FIVE§
1198—GUN-SHY BRIDE**
1204—HITCHED!**
1210—TWELVE-GAUGE GUARDIAN**
1234—BOOTS AND BULLETS^
1240—HIGH-CALIBER CHRISTMAS^
1246—WINCHESTER CHRISTMAS WEDDING^
1276—BRANDED‡
1282—LASSOED‡
1288—RUSTLED‡
1294—STAMPEDED‡
1335—CORRALLED‡
1353—WRANGLED‡
1377—JUSTICE AT CARDWELL RANCH
1413—CARDWELL RANCH TRESPASSER
1455—CHRISTMAS AT CARDWELL RANCH
1497—RESCUE AT CARDWELL RANCH†

*Whitehorse, Montana
§Whitehorse, Montana: The Corbetts
**Whitehorse, Montana: Winchester Ranch
^Whitehorse, Montana: Winchester Ranch Reloaded
‡Whitehorse, Montana: Chisholm Cattle Company
†Cardwell Cousins

Other titles by this author available in ebook format.

CAST OF CHARACTERS

Hayes Cardwell—The private detective showed up in Montana just in time to save a woman's life.

McKenzie Sheldon—Her realty business meant everything to her until the night she almost died.

Gus Thompson—The hotshot real estate agent thought he was irresistible to women, but the police suspect he was a stalker.

Eric Winters—How could he get arrested for the attempted abduction of the Realtor? All he did was go to a few open houses.

Bob Garwood—Was he just an innocent homebuyer? Or was he the man still stalking the Realtor?

Jason and Emily Mathews—They had their hearts set on having the best house and the best Realtor.

Dana Cardwell Savage—She loved having her cousin Hayes on Cardwell Ranch, even for a short visit.

Tag Cardwell—He was determined to move ahead on a Texas Boys Barbecue place in Big Sky, Montana. All he needed was his four brothers on board.

Chapter One

From the darkness, he heard the sound of high heels tapping quickly along the pavement, heading in his direction, and smiled. This could be the one.

If not, he would have to give it up for the night, something he couldn't bear doing. For days his need had been growing. He'd come here tonight because he couldn't put it off any longer—no matter how dangerous it was to hunt this close to home.

Since it had gotten dark, he'd been looking. He hated to think of the women he'd let get away, women in their tight skirts and low-cut blouses, women who'd just been asking for it.

But waiting for the right woman, he'd learned, was the smart thing to do. It took patience. Tonight, though, he found himself running short of it. He'd picked his favorite spot, the favorite spot of men like himself: a grocery-store parking lot at night. Once he'd parked next to her car—he knew it was a woman's car because she'd left her sunglasses on the dash and there was one of those cute air fresheners hanging from the mirror—he'd broken the bright light she'd parked under.

Now the area was cast in dark shadow—just the way he loved it. He doubted she would notice the lack of light—or him with his head down, pretending to be packing his groceries into the trunk of his large, expensive vehicle. Women were less afraid of a man who appeared to have money, he'd discovered.

At the sound of her approaching footfalls, he found it hard not to sneak a peek at her. *Patience.* This would be the one, he told himself. He already felt as if he knew her and could easily guess her story. She would have worked late, which was why she was still dressed as she had been this morning, in high heels. She wasn't pushing a cart so she wasn't shopping for her large family.

Instead, he guessed she was single and lived alone, probably in a nice condo since she drove a newer, pricier car—the kind independent, successful single women drove. By the sound of her footfalls, she carried only one small bag of groceries. He could already imagine his hands around her throat.

The footfalls grew closer.

He'd learned a long time ago not to act on impulse. Snatch the first one he saw and bad things happened. He had a scar to prove it. That run-in had almost cost him dearly. Not that she'd gotten away. He'd made sure of that. But she'd wounded him in more ways than one. It was why he'd come up with a set of rigorous guidelines he now followed to the letter. It was the reason, he told himself, that he'd never been caught.

He closed his eyes for a moment, imagining the look in her eyes when she realized she was about to die.

This woman *had* to be the right one because his need had grown to the point of urgency. He went over his guidelines, the memory of his only mistake still haunting him.

He wouldn't let himself be swayed by an alluring whiff of perfume. Nor would he risk a woman carrying anything that could be used as a weapon at a distance like an umbrella.

Then there was her hair and attire. It would surprise most women to know that what made her his target was her hairstyle. There was a reason women with short hair were not common prey of men like him. Give him a woman with a ponytail—a recent trend that filled him with joy—or a braid or even a bun—anything he could bury his fingers in and hold on for dear life.

Clothing was equally as important. She had to be wearing an outfit that would come off easily and quickly because he often didn't have a lot of time. Of course, he always carried a pair of sharp scissors, but a woman in a blouse and a skirt made his life so much easier, even with a blade handy.

Now as the sound of the high heels grew closer, he readied himself with growing anticipation. He was betting this one was wearing a nice short skirt and a button-up blouse. Tonight, he could even handle a matching jacket with the skirt. No blue jeans, though. They were such a pain to get off.

Her cell phone rang. She stopped walking. He groaned since if she'd been just a little closer, she would have already been in his trunk, her mouth duct taped as well as her wrists and ankles.

He cursed her cell phone even though it often made things easier for him. Women who were distracted—either digging in their purses for their keys or talking on their cell phones or unloading their groceries—were oblivious to the fact that he was already breathing down their necks.

He silently urged her phone call to end. Just a few more steps and he would grab her by the hair, overpower her and have her in the trunk of his car before she even knew what was happening. Once he got her to the place he had picked out down by the river...well, that was when the real fun would begin.

His next victim was still on the phone. She sounded upset, so upset that she'd stopped walking to take the call. She would be thinking about the call—not him right next to her car.

The call ended. She began to walk again, right toward him. He doubted she'd even noticed him bent over his car trunk, pretending to be taking care of his groceries.

He heard her vehicle beep as she unlocked it. Any moment she would walk within a few feet of him on his right. He would have only an instant to make his decision. An instant to see what she had in her hands, what she was wearing, how long her hair was. Even with his meticulous planning, there was always the chance that this could be the one woman who would surprise him. The one who would fight back. The one who would get away and ruin his perfect record.

His heart began to pound with excitement. He loved this part. None had ever gotten away—even the one who'd scarred him. He was too smart for them. They were like sheep coming down a chute to slaughter, he thought, as he looked up and saw her start past him.

Chapter Two

McKenzie Sheldon came out of the grocery store thinking about work. Not work, exactly, but one of the men at her office.

She was going to have to do something about Gus Thompson. The warnings she'd given him had fallen on deaf ears. The man had reached the point where he was daring her to fire him.

Shifting the single bag of groceries to her other arm, she began to dig for her keys when her cell phone rang. She stopped and pulled out her phone, saw it was her receptionist and said, "What's up, Cynthia?"

"You told me to call you if I was having any more problems."

McKenzie let out an angry breath. "Let me guess. *Gus.* What has he done now?" she asked with a disgusted sigh.

"I'm sorry, Ms. Sheldon, but he won't leave me alone. If I work late, *he* works late. He always insists on walking me to my car. I've told him that I'm not interested, but it seems to make him even more determined. I make excuses to avoid him, but—"

"I know. Trust me. It isn't anything you're doing."

"He scares me," she said, her voice breaking. "Tonight I looked out and he was waiting by my car. I'm afraid to try to go home."

She started to tell Cynthia that she didn't think Gus was dangerous, but what did she know? "Is he still out there?"

"I don't know." Her receptionist sounded close to tears.

"Call the police. Or if you want to wait, I can swing by—"

"I don't want you to have to do that. I'll call the police. I wanted to talk to you first. I didn't want to make any trouble."

"Don't worry about that. Gus is the one making the trouble. I promise you I'll take care of this tomorrow." She heard her receptionist make a scared sound. "Don't worry. I won't mention your name." She thought of the night she'd looked out her window at her condo. Gus had been sitting in his car across the street. He'd seen her and sped off, but she'd wondered how many other nights he'd been out there watching her house. "I should have fired him a long time ago."

"But he's your best salesman."

McKenzie let out a humorless laugh. "Hard to believe, isn't it?"

"Still, I wouldn't want to be blamed for him losing his job."

"You won't. Trust me. I have my own issues with him." She snapped the phone shut, angry with herself for letting things go on this long.

She had talked to Gus after that incident outside her house. He'd shrugged it off, made an excuse and she hadn't seen him again near her place. But that didn't mean he hadn't been more careful the next time. There was just no reining Gus in, she thought as she found her keys and started toward her car.

She wasn't looking forward to tomorrow. Gus wouldn't take being fired well. There would be a scene. She really hated scenes. But this was her responsibility as the owner of the agency. Maybe she should call him tonight and hire security until she could get Gus Thompson's desk cleaned out and the locks changed on the doors at the agency.

With a sigh, she hit the door lock on her key fob. The door on her SUV beeped. Out of the corner of her eye, she barely noticed the man parked next to her, loading his groceries. His back to her, he bent over the bags of groceries he'd put in his trunk as she walked past him.

She was thinking about Gus Thompson when the man grabbed her ponytail and jerked her off her feet. Shocked, she didn't make a sound. She didn't even drop her groceries as his arm clamped around her throat. Her only thought was: *this isn't happening.*

HAYES CARDWELL FELT his stomach growl as he walked down the grocery-store aisle. The place was empty at this hour of the night with just one clerk at the front, who'd barely noticed him when he walked in. The grocery was out of the way and it was late enough that most people had done their shopping, cooking and eating by now.

His plane had been delayed in Denver, putting him down in the Gallatin Valley much later than he'd hoped—and without any food for hours. He still had the drive to Big Sky tonight, one he wasn't looking forward to since he didn't know the highway.

Being from Texas, he wasn't used to mountains—let alone mountain roads. He was debating calling his brother Tag and telling him he would just get a motel tonight down here in the valley and drive up tomorrow in the daylight.

He snagged a bottle of wine to take to his cousin Dana Savage tomorrow and debated what he could grab to eat. The thought of going to a restaurant at this hour—and eating alone—had no appeal.

In the back of the store, he found a deli with premade items, picked himself up a sandwich and headed for the checkout. His Western boot soles echoed through the empty store. He couldn't imagine a grocery being this empty any hour of the day where he lived in Houston.

The checker was an elderly woman who looked as tired as he felt. He gave her a smile and two twenties. Her return smile was weak as she handed him his change.

"Have a nice night," she said in a monotone.

"Is there a motel close around here?"

She pointed down the highway to the south. "There's several." She named off some familiar chains.

He smiled, thanked her and started for the door.

MCKENZIE HAD TAKEN a self-defense class years ago. Living in Montana, she'd thought she would never need the training. A friend had talked her into it. The highlight of the course was that they'd always gone out afterward for hot-fudge sundaes.

That's all she remembered in the split second the man grabbed her.

He tightened his viselike grip on her, lifting her off her feet as he dragged her backward toward the trunk of his car. The man had one hand buried in her hair, his arm clamped around her throat. He was so much taller, she dangled like a rag doll from the hold he had on her. She felt one shoe drop to the pavement as she tried to make sense of what was happening.

Her mind seemed to have gone numb with her thoughts ricocheting back and forth from sheer panic to disbelief. Everything was happening too fast. She opened her mouth and tried to scream, but little sound came out with his arm pressed against her throat. Who would hear, anyway? There was *no* one.

Realization hit her like a lightning bolt. The parking lot was empty with only one other car at the opposite end of the lot. With such an empty lot, the man who'd grabbed her had parked right next to her. Also the light she'd parked under was now out. Why hadn't she noticed? Because she'd been thinking about Gus Thompson.

She saw out of the corner of her eye that the man had moved his few bags of groceries to one side of the trunk, making room for her. The realization that he'd been planning this sent a rush of adrenaline through her.

If there was one thing she remembered from the

defense class it was: *never let anyone take you to a second location.*

McKenzie drove an elbow into the man's side. She heard the air rush out of him. He bent forward, letting her feet touch the ground. She teetered on her one high heel for a moment then dropped to her bare foot to kick back and drive her shoe heel into his instep.

He let out a curse and, his hand still buried in her long hair, slammed her head into the side of his car. The blow nearly knocked her out. Tiny lights danced before her eyes. If she'd had any doubt before, she now knew that she was fighting for her life.

She swung the bag of groceries, glad she'd decided to cook from scratch rather than buy something quick. Sweet-and-sour chicken, her favorite from her mother's recipe, called for a large can of pineapple. It struck him in the side of the head. She heard the impact and the man's cry of pain and surprise. His arm around her neck loosened just enough that she could turn partway around.

McKenzie swung again, but this time, he let go of her hair long enough to block the blow with his arm. She went for his fingers, blindly grabbing two and bending them back as hard as she could.

The man let out a howl behind her, both of them stumbling forward. As she fell against the side of his car, she tried to turn and go for his groin. She still hadn't seen his face. Maybe if she saw his face, he would take off. Or would he feel he had to kill her?

But as she turned all she saw was the top of his baseball cap before he punched her. His fist connected with her temple. She felt herself sway then the grocery-store parking lot was coming up fast. She heard the twenty-ounce pineapple can hit and roll an instant before she joined it on the pavement.

From the moment he'd grabbed her, it had all happened in only a matter of seconds.

HAYES STEPPED OUT into the cool night air and took a deep breath of Montana. The night was dark and yet he could still see the outline of the mountains that surrounded the valley.

Maybe he would drive on up the canyon tonight, after all, he thought. It was such a beautiful June night and he didn't feel as tired as he had earlier. He'd eat the sandwich on his way and—

As he started toward his rented SUV parked by itself in the large lot, he saw a man toss what looked like a bright-colored shoe into his trunk before struggling to pick up a woman from the pavement between a large, dark car and a lighter-colored SUV. Both were parked some distance away from his vehicle in an unlit part of the lot.

Had the woman fallen? Was she hurt?

As the man lifted the woman, Hayes realized that the man was about to put her into the *trunk* of the car.

What the hell?

"Hey!" he yelled.

The man turned in surprise. Hayes only got a fleeting impression of the man since he was wearing a baseball cap pulled low and his face was in shadow in the dark part of the lot.

"Hey!" Hayes yelled again as he dropped his groceries. The wine hit the pavement and exploded, but Hayes paid no attention as he raced toward the man.

The man seemed to panic, stumbling over a bag of groceries on the ground under him. He fell to one knee and dropped the woman again to the pavement. Struggling to his feet, he left the woman where she was and rushed around to the driver's side of the car.

As Hayes sprinted toward the injured woman, the man leaped behind the wheel, started the car and sped off.

Hayes tried to get a license plate but it was too dark. He rushed to the woman on the ground. She hadn't moved. As he dropped to his knees next to her, the car roared out of the grocery parking lot and disappeared down the highway. He'd only gotten an impression of the make of the vehicle and even less of a description of the man.

As dark as it was, though, he could see that the woman was bleeding from a cut on the side of her face. He felt for a pulse, then dug out his cell phone and called for the police and an ambulance.

Waiting for 911 to answer, he noticed that the woman was missing one of her bright red high-heeled shoes. The operator answered and he quickly gave her the information. As he disconnected he looked down to see that the woman's eyes had opened. A sea of blue-green peered up at him. He felt a small chill ripple through him before he found his voice. "You're going to be all right. You're safe now."

The eyes blinked then closed.

Chapter Three

McKenzie's head ached. She gingerly touched the bandage and closed her eyes. "I'm sorry I can't provide you with a description of the man. I never saw his face." She'd tried to remember, but everything felt fuzzy and out of focus. She'd never felt so shaken or so unsure.

"Is the light bothering you?" the policewoman asked.

She opened her eyes as the woman rose to adjust the blinds on the hospital-room window. The room darkened, but it did nothing to alleviate the pain in her head. "It all happened so fast." Her voice broke as she remembered the gaping open trunk and the man's arm at her throat as she was lifted off her feet.

"You said the man was big."

She nodded, remembering how her feet had dangled above the ground. She was five feet six so he must have been over six feet. "He was…strong, too, muscular." She shuddered at the memory.

"You said he was wearing a baseball cap. Do you remember what might have been printed on it?"

"It was too dark." She saw again in her memory the pitch-black parking lot. "He must have broken the light because I would have remembered parking in such a dark part of the lot."

"Did he say anything?"

McKenzie shook her head.

"What about cologne?"

"I didn't smell anything." Except her own terror.

"The car, you said it was large and dark. Have you remembered anything else about it?"

"No." She hadn't been paying any attention to the car or the man and now wondered how she could have been so foolish.

The policewoman studied her for a moment. "We received a call last night from your receptionist about a man named Gus Thompson."

McKenzie felt her heart begin to pound. "Gus works for me. You aren't suggesting—"

"Is it possible the man who grabbed you was Gus Thompson?"

McKenzie couldn't speak for a moment. Gus was big. He also had to know, after numerous warnings, that she was ready to fire him. Or at least, he should have known. Could it have been him? Was it possible he hated her enough to want to hurt her? "I don't know."

"We found a car registered to him, a large, dark-colored Cadillac. Did you know he had this car?"

"No. But his mother recently died. I think he mentioned she'd left him a car."

"He never drove it to work?"

"No, not that I know of." Again, she hadn't been paying attention. She knew little about Gus Thompson because she'd chosen not to know any more than she had to. "I saw him parked outside my house one night. I spoke to him about it and I never saw him again, but I can't be sure he didn't follow me sometimes." She thought of one instance when she'd noticed him driving a few cars behind her. But Bozeman was small enough that it hadn't seemed all that odd at the time.

The policewoman raised a brow. "You never reported this?"

McKenzie tried to explain it to herself and failed. "I guess I thought he was annoying but harmless."

"Did you ever date him?"

"Good heavens, no."

"But Gus Thompson probably knows your habits, where you go after work, where you shop?"

She nodded numbly. Gus could have followed her many times and she wouldn't even have noticed. She'd been so caught up in making her business a success....

The policewoman closed her notebook. "We'll have a chat with Mr. Thompson and see where he was last night at the time of your attack."

"He wasn't at the office last night when you sent a patrolman over there?" she asked.

The policewoman shook her head. "He'd already left. Your receptionist was unsure when."

McKenzie felt a shiver, her mind racing. Could it have been Gus who'd attacked her? She swallowed, her throat raw and bruised from last night. Gus was big and strong and she knew he resented her. To think she'd almost reassured Cynthia that Gus wasn't dangerous. He could be more dangerous than she would have imagined.

"I used to work with his mother when she owned the agency," she said. "I inherited Gus. He is my best salesman, but I know he felt his mother should have left him the business and not sold it to me."

The policewoman nodded. "This could have been building for some time. We'll see what he has to say."

She had a thought. "I hit the man last night several times, but I'm not sure I did enough damage that it would even show." She described the ways she'd hit him.

"Don't worry. We'll check it out. In the meantime, you'll be safe here."

As the policewoman started to leave the room, McKenzie said, "The man who saved me last night..." She had a sudden flash. *You're safe now.* She blinked. "I'd like to get his name so I can thank him."

"He asked that his name be kept out of it."

She blinked. "Why?"

"There actually are people who don't want the notoriety. I can contact him if you like and see if he might have changed his mind. What I can tell you is that he just happened to fly in last night and stop at that grocery store on his way to see family. Fortunately for you."

"Yes. Fortunate." She had another flash of memory. Warm brown eyes filled with concern. *You're safe now.*

"The doctor said they're releasing you this afternoon. We're going to be talking to Mr. Thompson as soon as we can find him. Maybe going to the office isn't the best idea."

"I *have* to go into work. I was planning to fire Gus Thompson today. Even if he wasn't the man in the parking lot last night, I can't have him working for me any longer."

"Why don't you let us handle Mr. Thompson. We have your cell phone number. I'll call you when he and his personal items are out of your business. In the meantime, I would suggest getting new locks for your office and a restraining order for both yourself and your business."

She must have looked worried because the officer added, "You might want to stay with friends or relatives for a while."

"I have a client I need to see tomorrow south of here. I could go down there tonight and stay in a motel."

"I think that is a good idea," the policewoman said.

"LOOK WHAT THE cat dragged in," Tag Cardwell said as Hayes walked into the kitchen on the Cardwell Ranch. "We were getting ready to send the hounds out to track you down."

"Hey, cuz," Dana said as she got up from the table to give him a hug and offer him coffee. It was his first time meeting his cousin. She was pretty and dark like the rest of the Cardwells. As Tag had predicted, he liked her immediately. "We thought you'd be in last night."

"Ran into a little trouble," Hayes said and gladly took the large mug of coffee Dana handed him.

"That's Texas-speak for he met a woman," his brother joked.

Hayes told them what had happened and how it was after daylight before he left the police station. He didn't mention the strange feeling he'd had when the woman had opened her eyes.

"Is she all right?" Dana asked, clearly shocked.

For months, Tag had been talking up Montana and its low crime rate among all of its other amazing wonders.

"She regained consciousness in the ambulance. Last I heard she was going to be fine—at least physically. I'm not sure what a close call like that does to a person."

"Have the police found the man?" Dana asked, and hugged herself as if feeling a chill. Hayes thought about what his cousin had been through. She had personal experience with a psychopath who wanted to harm her.

"Unfortunately, the police don't have any leads. I wasn't able to get a license plate or even the model or make of the car the man was driving." He felt exhausted and stifled a yawn. He'd been going on nothing but adrenaline and caffeine since last night. "Hopefully, the woman will be able to give the cops a description so they can get the bastard."

"You look exhausted," Dana said. "I'll make you breakfast, then Tag will show you to your cabin. You two don't have anything planned until late afternoon, right?"

"Right," Tag said. "I'm taking my brother to see the restaurant space I found."

"Then get some rest, Hayes. We're having a steak fry tonight. Our fathers have said they are going to try to make it."

"That sounds great." He wasn't sure he was up to seeing his father. Harlan Cardwell had only been a passing figure in his life. Tag, who was the oldest, remembered him more than the other four of them. Harlan had come to Texas a few times, but his visits had been quick. Being the second to the youngest, Hayes didn't even remember his uncle Angus.

Hayes felt emotionally spent, sickened by what he'd witnessed last night and worried about the woman. He kept seeing her staring up at him with those eyes. He mentally shook himself as Dana put a plate of silver-dollar-sized pancakes with chokecherry syrup in front of him, along with a side of venison sausage and two sunny-side-up eggs.

He ate as if he hadn't eaten in days. As it was, he'd never gotten around to eating that sandwich he'd purchased at the grocery store last night. After he'd been plied with even more of Dana's amazing buttermilk pancakes, his brother walked him out to his rental SUV.

"So how are the wedding plans coming along?" he asked Tag as they got his gear and walked up a path behind the barn into the pines to his cabin.

He'd flown in a month early to talk his brother out of opening a Texas Boys Barbecue joint at Big Sky. The five brothers had started their first restaurant in a small old house in Houston. The business had grown by leaps and bounds and was now a multimillion-dollar corporation.

All five of them had agreed that they would keep the restaurants in Texas. But in December, Tag had come to Montana to spend Christmas with their father and had fallen in love with both Montana and Lily McCabe. Nothing like a woman and a little wilderness to mess with the best-laid plans.

It was now up to Hayes, as a spokesman for the other three brothers, to put Tag's feet firmly back on the ground and nip this problem in the bud.

"It's going to be an old-fashioned Western wedding," Tag was saying, his voice filled with excitement. "I can't wait for you to meet Lily. She's like no woman I have ever known."

Hayes didn't doubt it. He'd never seen his brother so happy. All of the brothers had the Cardwell dark good looks. Add to that their success, and women were often throwing themselves at one of them or another. Except for Jackson, none of them had found a woman they wanted to date more than a few times. They'd all become gun-shy after Jackson had bitten the bullet and gotten married—and quickly divorced after he found out his wife wanted nothing to do with their newborn son.

Hayes couldn't wait to meet this Lily McCabe to find out what kind of spell she'd cast over his brother—and possibly try to break it before the wedding.

GUS THOMPSON HAD never been so angry. The bitch had called the cops on him. He glanced toward the empty receptionist's desk at the front of the real-estate office. It didn't surprise him that Cynthia hadn't come in today. Stupid woman. Did she really think he would blame *her?*

No, he knew Cynthia didn't do *anything* without checking with her boss.

So where the hell *was* McKenzie Sheldon? No matter what was going on, she was usually at work before him every morning. *She must have had a rough night,* he thought with a smirk.

Where was everyone else? he wondered as he checked his watch. Had they heard about the police coming by his house last night?

When the front door opened, he turned in his office chair, the smirk still on his face since he'd been expecting McKenzie. He felt it fall away as he saw the cops. Hadn't it been enough that an officer had shown up at his door last night, questioning him about stalking the receptionist at the office? Now what?

"Mr. Thompson?" the policewoman asked. Her name tag read P. Donovan.

"Yes?" he asked, getting to his feet. He saw them look around the empty office.

"Are you here alone?"

"Everyone seems to be running late this morning," he said, and wondered why that was. Because they'd all been given a heads-up? Gus noticed the way both cops were looking at him, scrutinizing him as if he had horns growing out of his head.

"We'd like to ask you a few questions," the woman cop said. "Ms. Sheldon has asked us to first see that you remove your belongings from the premises."

"What?" he demanded. "The bitch is *firing* me? Has she lost her mind?"

P. Donovan's eyes went hard and cold at the word *bitch.* The word had just slipped out. He'd known McKenzie had it in for him, but he'd never dreamed she'd fire him.

"I'm her biggest-earning salesman," he said as if

there had been a mistake made and he hadn't made it. Neither responded. Instead, he saw the male cop looking around. "What?"

"Are there some boxes in the office you can put your belongings into?" the cop asked.

Hadn't either of them been listening? "She can't do this." Gus heard the hopelessness in his voice. He hated nothing worse than the feeling that came with it. He wanted to break something. Tear the place up. Then find McKenzie Sheldon and punch her in the face.

The male cop had gone into a storage room. He came back with two boxes. "Please take only those items belonging to you personally. We'll watch so we can tell Ms. Sheldon."

Gus gritted his teeth. McKenzie didn't even have the guts to face him. Well, this wasn't the last she'd see of him. He'd catch her in a dark alley. He started to shovel the top of the desk off into one of the boxes, but the male cop stopped him. T. Bradley, the name tag read.

"Leave any inventory you've been working on."

He grabbed up his coffee mug and threw it into the box. The couple of tablespoons of coffee left in the cup made a dark stain across the bottom. The same way McKenzie's blood was going to stain the spot where they met up again, he told himself.

His personal belongings barely filled one box. That realization made him sad and even angrier. This business should have been his. When he was a boy, he used to sleep on the floor of the main office when his mother had to work late. This place had been more like home than home during those years when she'd been growing the business.

"Is that everything?" P. Donovan asked.

He didn't bother to answer as T. Bradley asked for his key to the building.

"Ms. Sheldon has taken out a restraining order against you," the cop said. "Are you familiar with the way they work?"

He looked at the cop. "Seriously? Do I look like someone who is familiar with restraining orders?"

"You are required to stay away from Ms. Sheldon and this building. If you harass her—"

"I get it," he snapped, and handed over his key. As he started toward the door, T. Bradley blocked his way.

"We're going to need you to come down to the police station with us to answer a few more questions."

"About what?" The receptionist, bloody hell. "Look, I haven't done anything that any red-blooded American male doesn't do. I like women." He realized they were staring at him. "Come on. She liked it or she wouldn't have led me on."

"Whom are you referring to?" P. Donovan asked.

He frowned. "Cynthia. The receptionist. She was threatening to call the cops last night, but I didn't really think she'd do it. Why would you ask me that? Who else called the cops on me?"

"Didn't she ask you to leave her alone?" the woman cop asked.

He shrugged. "I thought she was just playing hard to get."

"What about Ms. Sheldon? Did you also think she was just playing hard to get?" T. Bradley asked.

Gus closed his eyes and sighed. So she'd told them about that time she'd caught him in her neighborhood. "There's no law against sitting in your car on a public street. I didn't even realize she lived in the area. I was looking at the house down the block, okay?" Not even he could make the lie sound convincing.

"Let's go," P. Donovan said and led him out of the building as if he were a criminal. In the small parking lot, he saw his colleagues waiting in their vehicles for the police to take him away.

He wanted to kill McKenzie.

"Please open the trunk of your car, Mr. Thompson," T. Bradley said as Gus started to put the box in the backseat.

"Why?" he demanded.

"Just please open it," P. Donovan said.

He thought they probably needed a warrant or something, but he didn't feel like making things any worse. He cursed under his breath as he moved to the back of the vehicle and, using his key, opened the trunk. It was empty, so he put the box in it. "Satisfied?"

It wasn't until T. Bradley rode with him to the police station and they had him inside in an interrogation room that they demanded to know where he'd been last night after he'd left the office.

"We know you didn't go straight home," P. Donovan said. "Where did you go?"

So much for being Mr. Nice Guy. Through gritted teeth, Gus said, "I want to speak with my attorney. *Now.*"

Chapter Four

He'd failed.

Failed.

The word knocked around in his mind, hammering at him until he could barely think.

You got too cocky last night, you and your perfect record.

It wasn't his fault. It was the woman's. The fool woman's and that cowboy with the Southern accent who'd rescued her.

That rationale didn't make him feel any better. He'd had one woman who'd fought back before, he thought, tracing a finger across the scar on his neck. But he hadn't let her get away and she'd definitely paid for what she'd done to him.

The possibility of not only failure, but getting caught was what made it so exciting. He loved the rush. But he also loved outsmarting everyone and getting away with it. Last night should have gone off without a hitch. The woman was the perfect choice. He'd done everything right. If he hadn't had to knock her out… Even so, a few more seconds and he would have had her in the trunk. Then it was a short drive to the isolated spot he'd found by the river.

His blood throbbed, running hot through his veins, at the thought of what he would have done to her before he dumped her body in the Gallatin River. He had to kill them for his own protection. If he were ever a suspect, there couldn't be any eyewitnesses.

Except last night he'd left behind *two* eyewitnesses—the woman and the cowboy. Had either of them gotten a good look at him or his vehicle? He didn't know.

A costly mistake. He mentally beat himself for not waiting until he could leave town before grabbing another one. The northwest was like a huge marketplace, every small town had perfect spots for the abduction and the dumping of the bodies. Small-town sheriff's offices were short on manpower. Women weren't careful because people felt safe in small towns.

Also, he had the perfect job. He traveled, putting a lot of miles on the road every year with different vehicles at his disposal. He saw a lot of towns, learned their secrets at the cafés and bars, felt almost at home in the places where he'd taken women.

But last night, after a few weeks unable to travel, he'd been restless. The ache in him had reached a pitch. His need had been too strong. He'd never taken a woman in his hometown. One wouldn't hurt, he'd thought. No, he hadn't been thinking at all. He'd taken a terrible chance and look what had happened.

He gingerly touched the side of his head where she'd hit him with whatever canned good had been in her grocery bag. Fortunately, other than being painful, the bruise didn't show through his thick hair. His shin was only slightly skinned from where she'd nailed him with her high heel and his fingers ached. No real visible signs of what she'd done to him. Not that he didn't feel it all and hate her for hurting him.

It could have been so much worse. He tried to console himself with that, but it wasn't working. The woman had made a fool out of him. It didn't make any difference that he shouldn't have gone for so long since the last one. But it had begun to wear on him. Otherwise, he would never have taken one this close to home. He would never have taken the chance.

The television flickered. He glanced up as the news came on. This was why he couldn't let them live, he thought, as he watched the story about a botched abduction at the small, out-of-the-way grocery store the night before. He waited for the newsman to mention the woman's name and put her on camera to tell of her heroic rescue by the cowboy. He wanted to see the fear in her eyes—but more than anything, he needed her *name*.

The news station didn't put her on air. Nor did they give her name or the cowboy's who'd rescued her.

Furious, he tried several other stations. He'd gotten a good look at her last night after he'd punched her and had her on the ground.

But he foolishly hadn't bothered to take down her car license number or grab her purse. He hadn't cared who the woman was. She'd been nobody to him. But now he was desperate to know everything about her. All the others, he'd learned about them after their bodies were found. It had never mattered who they were.

They'd already served their purpose. Now it was inconceivable that he didn't know the name of the only woman who'd ever gotten away.

Without her name, he wouldn't be able to find her and finish what he'd started.

STANDING IN THE hospital room half-dressed, McKenzie tried to still her trembling fingers. The morning sun was blinding. Her head still ached, but she'd kept that from the doctor. After the police had left, he'd made her spend the night in the hospital for observation. Today, though, she had to get back to work. It was the only thing that could keep her mind off what had happened. Worse, what could have happened if someone hadn't stopped the man.

"Let me," her sister said and stepped to her to button the blouse.

She stood still, letting her big sister dress her—just as she had as a child. "Thank you. I wouldn't have called but I needed a change of clothing before I could leave the hospital."

Shawna shook her head. She was the oldest of nine and had practically raised them all since her mother had been deathly ill with each pregnancy, especially with her last baby—McKenzie.

"Mac, I would expect you to call because I'm your *sister* and, after what you've been through, you need your family."

She didn't like needing anyone, especially her big sister. "I didn't want to be any trouble."

Her sister laughed. "You have always been like this."

She straightened McKenzie's collar. "You've never wanted to be any trouble. So independent. And stubborn. There. You look fine."

She didn't feel fine. From an early age, just as her sister had said, she had been fiercely independent, determined to a fault, wanting to do everything herself and driven to succeed at whatever she did. She was still that way. Nothing had changed—and yet, after last night, everything felt as if it had.

It was as if the earth was no longer solid under her feet. She felt off-balance, unsure—worse, afraid.

"Are you sure you're ready to leave the hospital?" Shawna asked, studying her.

"The doctor says my head will hurt for a while, but that I should be fine. I need to get to the office and reassure everyone. I had to fire one of my employees today." She swallowed, her sore throat again reminding her of the man's arm around her neck. Had it been Gus Thompson? The thought made her blood run cold. "I'm sure everyone is upset."

"You can't worry about them right now. You need to think about yourself. Just go home and rest. I can stop by your office—"

"No, this is something I need to do myself." She saw her sister's disappointment. Shawna lived to serve. "But thank you so much for bringing me a change of clothes."

"What do you want me to do with the clothes you were wearing?" she asked, picking up the bag. Her pretty new suit was blood-splattered from the now bandaged head wound. So was the blouse she'd been wearing.

"Throw them away. I don't want them."

She felt her older sister's gaze on her. "There doesn't seem to be anything wrong with the suit or the blouse. Once I get them clean… It seems a shame—"

"Then drop them off at Goodwill."

Her sister nodded. "Are the police giving you protection?"

"They really can't do that. Anyway, there's no need. If it was someone I know, then they don't believe he'll try anything again with them involved. And if it was random…then the man could be miles from here by now."

Shawna didn't look any more convinced than McKenzie felt. "I guess they know best."

"I'm going to stay in Big Sky tonight. I have a client I need to see up there this afternoon so I'll spend the night and come back tomorrow."

"Do you want me to go home with you to your condo and wait while you pack?"

She thought of her empty condo. "No. That's not necessary." But even as she said it, she was already dreading facing it alone. "I know you need to get back to your job." She stepped to her sister and hugged her. Shawna had never married. But she kept busy with three jobs as if needing to fill every hour of her day doing for others.

"You've done enough," McKenzie said. Her big sister had always been there for her from as far back as she could remember. It made her feel guilty because she felt her sister had been robbed of her childhood. Shawna had been too busy raising their mother's babies.

"If you need anything…"

"I know." Sometimes she felt as if Shawna had made

a life in Montana so she could watch over her. All the other siblings had left, stretching far and wide around the world. Only she and Shawna had stayed in the Gallatin Valley after their parents had passed.

But her big sister couldn't always protect her. Before last night, McKenzie would have said she could protect herself. Last night had proved how wrong she was about that.

GUS THOMPSON WOULD never forget the humiliation he'd been put through at the police department. "Don't you know who I am?" he'd finally demanded.

They had looked at him blankly.

"My photo is all over town on real-estate signs. I am number one in this valley. I sell more property than any of the hundreds of agents out there. I'm *somebody* and I don't have to put up with this ridiculous questioning."

"You still haven't told us where you were last night." The woman cop was starting to really tick him off.

He looked to his attorney, who leaned toward him and whispered that he should just tell them since it would be better than their finding out later. "I went for a drive. I do that sometimes to relax."

"Did you happen to drive by the River Street Market?"

"I don't remember. I was just driving."

"We searched your car… Actually, the car that is still registered to your mother, and we found a gas receipt." The woman cop again. "You were within a quarter mile of the grocery last night only forty-two minutes before the incident involving Ms. Sheldon."

"So what?" he snapped. "Aren't you required to tell me what I'm being accused of? Someone steal McKenzie's groceries?"

"Someone attacked and attempted to abduct Ms. Sheldon."

"Trust me. The guy would have brought her back quick enough." Neither cop smiled, let alone laughed. He raked a hand through his hair. "Why would I try something like that in a grocery-store parking lot when I could have abducted McKenzie Sheldon any night right at the office?"

His attorney groaned and the two cops exchanged a look.

"Come on," Gus said. "I didn't do anything to her. I swear." But he sure wanted to *now.* Wasn't it enough that she'd fired him? Apparently not. She wanted to *destroy* him. Something like this could hang over his head for years—unless they caught the guy who really attacked her. What was the chance of that happening? Next to none when they weren't even out looking for him.

He pointed this out to the cops. "Get out there and find this guy. It's the only way I can prove to you that I'm innocent."

They both looked at him as if they suspected he was far from innocent. But they finally let him go.

Once outside the police station, Gus realized he didn't know what he was going to do now. Of course, another Realtor would hire him. The top salesman in Gallatin Valley? Who wouldn't?

Unless word got around about Sheldon's attack—

and his firing. Everyone would think it was because he was the one who'd attacked McKenzie. How long would it take before everyone knew? He groaned. Gossip moved faster than an underpriced house, especially among Realtors.

McKenzie Sheldon better hope she hadn't just destroyed his reputation—*and* his career.

"I'M ANXIOUS FOR you to see the building I found for the very first Big Sky Texas Boys Barbecue," Tag said later that afternoon. "The Realtor is going to meet us there in a few minutes."

Hayes had taken a long nap after the breakfast Dana had made for him. He'd awakened to the dinner bell. Dana was one heck of a cook. Lunch included chicken-fried elk steaks, hash browns, carrots from the garden and biscuits with sausage gravy.

"This is the woman who should be opening a restaurant," Hayes said to his cousin.

"Thanks, but no, thanks," Dana said. "I have plenty to do with four small children." As if summoning them, the four came racing into the kitchen along with their father, Hud, the local marshal. The kids climbed all over their father as Dana got him a plate. It amazed him how much noise kids seven to two could make.

Tag's fiancée, Lily McCabe, came in looking as if she was already family. She declined lunch, saying she'd already eaten, but she pulled up a chair. Introductions were made and five minutes later, Hayes could see why his brother had fallen in love with the beautiful and smart brunette.

"We'd better get going," Tag said, checking his watch. He gave Lily a kiss then rumpled each child's hair as he headed for the door. Hayes followed, even though there was no purpose in seeing this building his brother had found for the restaurant.

They weren't opening a barbecue place in Big Sky. He wasn't sure how he was going to break it to his brother, though.

The road from the ranch crossed a bridge over the Gallatin River. This morning it ran crystal clear, colorful rocks gleaming invitingly from the bottom. Hayes watched the river sweep past, the banks dotted with pines and cottonwoods, and wished they were going fishing, instead.

At Highway 191, Tag turned toward Big Sky and Hayes got his first good look at Lone Mountain. The spectacular peak glistened in the sun. A patch of snow was still visible toward the top where it hadn't yet melted. This morning, when he'd driven to the ranch, the top of the peak had been shrouded in clouds.

"Isn't it beautiful?" Tag said.

"It is." All of the Montana he'd seen so far was beautiful. He could understand why his brother had fallen in love with the place. And with Lily McCabe.

"Lily was nervous about meeting you earlier," Tag said now, as if reading his mind. He turned toward Lone Mountain and what made up the incorporated town of Big Sky.

Hayes could see buildings scattered across a large meadow, broken only by pines and a golf course. "Why would she be nervous?"

"She was afraid my brothers wouldn't like her."

"What is the chance of that?" Hayes said. He had to admit that Lily hadn't been what he'd expected. She was clearly smart, confident and nice. He hadn't found any fault with her. In fact, it was blatantly clear why Tag was head over heels in love with the woman.

But Lily had reason to be nervous. She was backing Tag on the restaurant idea. A math professor at Montana State University in Bozeman, she didn't want to move to Texas with her future husband. A lot was riding on what Tag's brothers decided. Their not wanting a Montana barbecue place had nothing to do with liking or disliking Lily.

"Is she going to meet us at the restaurant building site?" Hayes asked, wondering how involved the bride-to-be was planning to be in the barbecue business. After the fiasco with Jackson's wife, the brothers had decided no wives would ever own interest in the corporation. They couldn't chance another ugly divorce that could destroy Texas Boys Barbecue. Or a *marriage* that would threaten the business, for that matter.

"No, she's doing wedding planning stuff," Tag said. "Who knew all the things that are involved in getting married?"

"Yes, who knew," Hayes agreed as his brother turned into a small, narrow complex. He saw the For Sale sign on a cute Western building stuck back in some pine trees and knew it must be the one his brother had picked out.

"Good, McKenzie is already here," Tag said just an instant before Hayes saw her.

He stared in shock at the woman he'd seen the night before. Only last night McKenzie had been lying at his feet outside a grocery store as her would-be abductor sped away.

Chapter Five

"Hayes, meet McKenzie Sheldon, Realtor extraordinaire," Tag said. "McKenzie, this is my brother Hayes."

McKenzie smiled, but she wasn't sure how convincing it was. Her sister had tried to talk her into moving this meeting to another day. Maybe she should have listened. She hadn't felt like herself all day.

While she'd tried to put what had happened last night out of her mind, she kept reliving it. Now she felt jumpy and realized it had been a mistake to take the attitude "business as usual" today.

But she couldn't bear the thought of hanging out at the condo all day when she knew nothing could take her mind off last night in that case. Her first stop had been the office where she'd assured everyone that Gus Thompson would no longer be a problem. While she was there, the locksmith came and changed all the locks, which seemed to reassure some and make others at the office even more nervous since Gus hadn't gotten along with any of his coworkers.

Then she'd gone to her condo, packed quickly for overnight and driven to Big Sky to meet her client.

She'd worn a plain suit with a scarf to cover the bruises on her neck, but the gash on her temple where the man had slugged her still required a bandage if she hoped to hide the stitches.

As she caught her reflection in the empty building window, she saw with a start that she looked worse than she'd thought. How else could she explain Hayes Cardwell's reaction to her? His eyes had widened in alarm as he put out his hand.

He looked like a man who'd just seen a ghost. He'd *recognized* her. How was that possible when he'd only flown in yesterday?

"Pleased to meet you, Ms. Sheldon."

Tag had told her that his brothers shared more than a love of barbecue. The resemblance was amazing. Like Tag, Hayes Cardwell had the dark hair and eyes, had the wonderful Southern accent and was handsome as sin.

She thought of Ted Bundy as she took Hayes Cardwell's large hand, hers disappearing inside it, and saw his dark gaze go to the bandage on her head. "I had a little accident last night."

"You're all right, though?" He still held her hand. She could feel herself trembling and feared he could, too.

She put on her best smile. "Fine." Then she finally met his gaze.

His eyes were a deep brown and so familiar that it sent a shudder through her. Even though she'd told her sister that there was nothing to worry about, she was well aware that the man who'd attacked her last night could be closer than she thought.

HE'D STAYED HOME from work saying he didn't feel well, even though he knew that might look suspicious if he was ever a suspect. But he was too anxious and upset over last night to go to work today.

There'd been nothing of use in the morning paper, only a short few paragraphs.

> Police say a man tried to abduct a 28-year-old woman about 10:35 p.m. last night in the River Street Market parking lot.
>
> The man attacked the woman as she came out of the market and attempted to put her into the trunk of his vehicle. He is described as over six feet with a muscular build. He was wearing a dark-colored baseball cap and driving a newer-model large car, also dark in color.
>
> If anyone has information, they should contact the local police department.

He knew he should be glad that the information was just as useless to the police. She hadn't gotten a good look at him, which was great unless they had some reason to withhold that information. That aside, nothing in the news was helping him find the woman.

Too restless to stay in the house, he decided to go for a walk in his northside neighborhood to clear his head. The houses were smaller on this side of town, many of them having been remodeled when the boom in housing came through years before.

House prices had dropped with the mortgage fiasco, but so many people wanted to live in his valley that prices had never reached the lows they had elsewhere. He was glad he hadn't been tricked into selling his house for top dollar. He could have found himself in a house he couldn't afford. Instead, his small, comfortable home was paid for since he lived conservatively.

Everything about his lifestyle looked normal on paper. He'd attended Montana State University right there in Bozeman. He'd bought a house after he graduated with a degree in marketing and had gone to work for a local company. He was an exemplary employee, a good neighbor, a man who flew under the radar. If caught, everyone who knew him would be shocked and say they never would have suspected him of all people.

As he walked around his neighborhood, he saw that more houses were for sale. It made him upset to think that his older neighbors were dying off because more college students would be moving in. Constant temptation, he thought with a groan.

He promised himself the next time he took a woman it would be in another town. Even better, another state. He couldn't take the chance so close to home ever again. If there *was* another time. Last night's botched abduction had left him shaken. She'd jinxed things for him. If he didn't find the woman and fix this—

At a corner he hadn't walked past in some time, he saw that another house had gone on the market. But that wasn't what made him stumble to a stop next to the strip of freshly mown lawn.

There she was! He could never forget that face and now there she was. Right there on the real-estate sign in the yard, smiling up at him as if daring him to come after her.

McKenzie Sheldon of M.K. Sheldon Realty.

"ARE YOU ALL RIGHT?"

McKenzie nodded, even though she was far from all right. Did she really think she recognized this man? She hadn't seen the face of the man who'd tried to abduct her so she couldn't have seen his eyes. This man's eyes were…familiar and yet she'd never met him before, had she? Would she look at every man she met and think he was the one who'd attacked her?

Hayes Cardwell was staring at her with concern and something else in his expression. Compassion?

It was the very last thing she needed right now. Tears welled in her eyes. She felt lightheaded and groped for the wall behind her for support.

"If you'd prefer to do this some other time," Hayes said.

She shook her head. "No, I'm fine. It must have been something I ate." In truth, she hadn't eaten anything since the day before. No wonder she felt lightheaded. But she'd toughened it out through worse, she told herself, remembering when she'd taken on the agency.

Tag Cardwell hadn't seemed to notice her no doubt odd behavior. He was busy looking in the windows of the building, anxious to get inside and show his brother the space.

"I think you're going to like this location for your restaurant," she said, turning away from Hayes Cardwell's dark, intent gaze and what she saw there. "Let me show you. It's perfect for what you have in mind."

Her fingers shook so hard, she didn't think she was going to be able to put the key in the lock. A large, sun-tanned hand reached around her and gently took the keys from her.

"Let me do that," Hayes said. His voice was soft, his Southern accent comforting and almost familiar.

She was going mad. She could smell his male scent along with the soap he'd used to shower that morning. He was a big man—like the man last night who'd attacked her. She touched her bruised throat and closed her eyes against the terrifying memory.

He opened the door and she stumbled in and away from him. Her cell phone rang and she was startled to see that it was the police department.

"I need to take this. Please have a look around." She scooted past Hayes and back outside, leaving the two men alone inside what had been a restaurant only months ago. Her phone rang again. She sucked in a deep breath of the June mountain air and, letting it out, took the call. As she did, she prayed the man had been caught. She couldn't keep living like this.

"Ms. Sheldon?" the policewoman asked.

"Yes?"

"I spoke to the man who intervened last night during your attack. He still would prefer to remain anonymous."

"You're sure he wasn't involved?"

"Involved? No. The clerk at the store was a witness. He was leaving the store when he saw the abductor trying to lift you into the trunk of his car. The man saved your life."

"So why is this so-called hero so determined to remain anonymous?"

"As I told you, he's in town visiting relatives. He doesn't want the notoriety. But I can assure you, we checked him out. He just happened to be in the right place at the right time last night."

McKenzie felt as if she could breathe a little easier. "I'm sorry he won't let me thank him, but I certainly appreciate what he did. Is there any word on...?"

"No, but we are looking at Gus Thompson. We brought him in. He doesn't have an alibi for last night."

"You really think it was him?" She shuddered, remembering. He was about the right size and he *had* acted more than a little creepy in the past.

Behind her, the door opened. She heard Tag and his brother come out.

"Thank you for letting me know," she said to the patrolwoman and disconnected. "So what do you think?" she asked, but one look at their faces and she knew Hayes hadn't liked the place.

Tag had been so excited about the building. She could get it for him at a good price since the owner was anxious to sell. But she could see that Hayes was far from sold.

"We can't really make a decision until all my brothers see the place," Tag said. Hayes said nothing.

She could feel the tension between the two men. "Well, let me know. This property won't stay on the market long. I'll lock up." She moved past Hayes to turn out the light and lock the door.

When she came back out, the brothers were leaving. She shivered as she felt someone watching her. Her gaze shot to Hayes, but he was looking off toward the mountains and his brother was busy driving.

I'm losing my mind. Hayes Cardwell wasn't her attacker. So why, when she thought of his brown eyes, did some memory try to fight to surface?

GUS THOMPSON WAS going to see McKenzie no matter what anyone said. When he'd come out of the police station and climbed into his vehicle, he hadn't known where to go or what to do. He had to save his career, and McKenzie was the only one who could do that.

Restraining order or not, he *would* see her.

He had racked his brain, trying to remember where she said she had a showing today. Something about a listing in Big Sky. A former restaurant. He'd quickly checked to see what commercial restaurant space was under the multiple listings at Big Sky and laughed out loud when he'd found the restaurant with ease.

It didn't take much to find out what time she was showing the place. He'd called the office, changed his voice and pretended to be the person she was showing the restaurant to. Within minutes, he'd found out that McKenzie would be at the restaurant this afternoon at two to meet the Cardwells.

For a few minutes after he'd hung up, he'd tried to talk himself out of driving up to Big Sky. The last thing he needed was for her to call the police before she heard him out. It appalled him that she thought she could just fire him and he'd go away. Well, she was dead wrong about that.

Unfortunately, the forty-mile drive had taken longer than he'd expected. Summer traffic. He'd forgotten about the damned tourists so he hadn't been able to beat McKenzie to the restaurant—which had been his intent.

Fifty minutes later, he'd parked next to a small grocery in a space where he had a good view of the restaurant with the M.K. Realty sign out front. He'd arrived in time to see two men pull up in an SUV only moments after McKenzie.

He'd been forced to wait, telling himself it might work out better. He would grab her after her showing. He could get a lay of the land before he did anything stupid. More stupid, he thought, thinking of Cynthia, the receptionist. She wasn't even that cute.

While he had no patience for waiting, he was surprised when the showing only took a matter of minutes. He had to laugh. Boy, had that not gone well. And now McKenzie had just lost her best salesman. She would definitely regret firing him, probably already did.

He saw his chance when the two men McKenzie had shown the property to got into their SUV and drove away. The restaurant location was somewhat secluded, separated from the other businesses by pine trees.

Once he got her alone, she'd be forced to listen to what he had to say.

As he started his vehicle, planning to park behind her car so she couldn't get away, he saw her looking around. Was she worried he might show up? Or was she looking for the man who'd attacked her last night? Her gaze skimmed over him in his vehicle where he still sat, motor running. He looked away, glad he'd driven his silver SUV that looked like everyone else's around here.

When he'd dared take a peek again, she was headed for her car. He couldn't let her just drive away. His best chance of talking to her was here rather than back in Bozeman.

Gus shifted the SUV into gear. He told himself all he wanted to do was tell her what he thought of her firing him, of accusing him of attacking her, of treating him like an employee rather than appreciating what he did for M.K. Realty.

He just needed to have his say. He wasn't stupid enough to touch her. Or threaten her. He had the right to have the last word. She couldn't just get rid of him in such a humiliating way and think he was going to let it pass.

But as he'd started to drive up the road to the empty restaurant, another vehicle pulled in and parked next to her car. Annoyed, he saw that he would have to wait again. He hadn't come all this way to give up. He killed his engine with a curse. If he couldn't get to her now, then soon. She would hear him out, one way or another.

MCKENZIE HATED THE scared feeling she had as she hurried to her car. Her gaze took in the activity lower on the hillside. She told herself she'd just imagined someone watching her. Down the road, there were families in vans with laughing and screaming children, older people trying to park in front of one of the small businesses that dotted the meadow, a young couple heading into the grocery store.

Everywhere she looked there were people busy with their own lives. It was June in Montana, a time when in Big Sky, it seemed everyone was on vacation. No one had any reason to be watching her.

Still, she gripped her keys in her fist until her hand ached as she neared her car. She wanted to run but she was afraid that like a mad dog, the person watching her would give chase. She couldn't see anyone watching her and yet the hair rose on the back of her neck. The afternoon sun had sunk behind Lone Mountain. Shadows moved on the restless breeze through the pines next to the building.

Fear was making her paranoid, but she couldn't shake off the feeling that the man from last night hadn't left town. Nor had he forgotten about her.

She reached the car, opened the door and climbed in, fumbling in a panic to get the door locked. The moment she did, she realized she hadn't looked in the backseat. Her gaze shot to the rearview mirror. She swiveled around. The backseat was empty.

Hot tears burned down her cheeks. She began to shake uncontrollably.

At the sound of a vehicle approaching, she brushed at her tears and tried to pull herself together. She was trying to put the key into the ignition, when the tap on her side window made her jump.

Her head swung around and she found herself looking up at Hayes Cardwell. She cursed herself. He would see that she'd been crying. She felt a wave of embarrassment and anger at herself.

"Are you all right?" Hayes mouthed.

She lowered the window a few inches. "I—"

"I know. That's why I came back. There's something I need to tell you."

"If it's about the restaurant space—"

"The police called me and asked me again if I would mind if they told you that I was the man who found you last night at the grocery store."

She felt her eyes widen in alarm. "You—" The brown eyes. A flicker of memory. *You're safe now.*

"I can't imagine what you're going through, that's all I wanted to say. I was worried about you. But I didn't want you thinking…"

She nodded, unable to speak around the lump in her throat. He'd seen her reaction to him. It was the reason he'd decided to tell her. He didn't want her thinking he was the one who'd hurt her. Her eyes burned again with tears.

"Call the police. I understand why you would suspect me. I'll be over here when you finish if you want to talk or anything." He stepped away from her car.

She put the window up and dug out her phone. When the patrolwoman came on the line she asked, "The man who saved me last night? Was his name Hayes Cardwell?"

"So he *did* contact you."

"It's true?"

"Yes. He and his brothers own a chain of—"

"Barbecue restaurants in Texas."

"That's right. He also works as a private investigator in Houston. Like I said, we checked him out thoroughly. Plus, we have an eyewitness who saw him rescue you."

"Thank you." She disconnected and, pulling herself together, climbed out of the car.

Hayes was standing at the edge of the building, looking toward the Gallatin River. In the afternoon sun, the surface of the water shimmered like gold. The scent of pine wafted through the June air. There was nothing like Montana in the summer.

"I'm so sorry I suspected you." He'd never know how much. "The police told me that I owe my life to you. Thank you."

He turned to look at her, kindness in his dark eyes. "No, please, don't feel bad. I didn't tell you so you could—"

"Thank you?"

He shrugged, looking shy. "I just happened to be in the grocery store."

"I didn't mean to make you uncomfortable."

"I'm afraid I'm the one who made you uncomfortable. I apologize for staring earlier. I was just so surprised to see you again."

She nodded and touched her bruised neck, remembering the man's arm around her throat and fighting for breath.

"Are you sure you should be working this soon after what you've been through?" he asked.

"I needed to keep my mind off...everything."

"Is it working?"

She gave him a weary smile. "No," she said and

looked away. "I've felt jumpy all day and I haven't been able to shake the feeling that someone is…watching me." She glanced around again, the feeling still strong. She shivered, even though the afternoon was warm.

What if the man from last night wasn't through with her? Wasn't that what had been in the back of her mind all day?

HAYES LOOKED PAST her. He saw people coming and going at a nearby small business complex. No one seemed to be looking in this direction, though.

"You say you feel as if someone's watching you?"

She nodded. "I know I'm just being paranoid—"

"Your best defense is your instincts. Don't discount them."

She stared at him and tried to swallow the lump in her throat. "You think he'll come after me again?"

"I don't know. Is there any way he knows who you are?"

"I… The police think it might be a man I worked with. I fired him today. I have a restraining order—"

Hayes scoffed at that. "Restraining orders can't protect you from a predator. Where are you staying?"

"I checked into a motel up here for the night—"

He shook his head. "My cousin Dana owns a ranch not far from here. She recently built several guest cabins. I'd feel better if you'd consider staying there—at least until the police have a chance to catch this man." Hayes knew from experience that there was little chance they would catch him—unless he did turn out to be this man she'd fired.

"I couldn't impose."

"You wouldn't be imposing, trust me. My cousin Dana loves a full house and you would be doing me a favor."

She cocked a brow. "How's that?"

"I wouldn't have to worry about you the whole time I'm in town."

McKenzie smiled. It was a nice smile, a real one, and he was suddenly aware of how attractive she was. She had long hair the color of caramel. Most of it was pulled up with a clip at the nape of her neck, but a few strands had escaped, framing a face that was all girl-next-door—from the sprinkling of freckles that dusted her cheeks and nose to the wide-set tropical-blue eyes. But it was her mouth that kept drawing his attention. It was full, her lips a pale pink. Right now she worried at her lower lip with her teeth.

She had the kind of mouth a man fantasized about kissing.

He roped in his thoughts, telling himself not to make a big deal out of this coincidence. But he couldn't shake the memory of the first time he'd looked into her eyes. And now here she was, Tag's real-estate agent. As a private detective, he'd never bought into coincidences. This was definitely one that had him thrown off-balance.

"You'll like my family and you'll be safe." After that, he didn't want to think about it. Maybe the police would get lucky and catch the man.

"Are you sure about this? I know you didn't want to be involved..."

"I *am* involved," he said and smiled. Maybe more

involved than he should be, he thought. "Do you need to stop by your motel to cancel your reservation?"

"I hadn't checked in yet. I can call."

"Why don't you follow me to the ranch, then, and meet the Cardwells. Trust me. You're going to love them and feel at home there."

"WHAT?" TAG SAID as they stood in the ranch house living room later. "McKenzie is the woman you saved?"

Hayes nodded.

"Talk about a small world. So you decided to bring her back to the ranch?"

"Look, I know you're upset with me about the restaurant—"

"I'm just trying to understand what you're thinking. Since you're only going to be here a couple of days, how do you intend to keep this woman safe?"

"I don't know what I was thinking, okay? She was scared. When I went back and found her, she was losing it, all right? She thought someone was watching her."

Tag looked skeptical.

"I think she was probably imagining it, but she's terrified this predator will come for her again. Who wouldn't be?"

"You did the right thing," Dana said from the doorway. "I'm glad you brought her here. It isn't like we don't have plenty of room. I put her in the cabin next to yours, Hayes. She can stay as long as she wants."

"With the wedding coming up July Fourth—"

Dana cut Tag off. "Your brothers can always bunk together if they haven't caught the man who attacked her by the time Jackson, Austin and Laramie arrive. I told her she is welcome to stay as long as she wants to and that is that."

Tag didn't look happy about it. "It makes it pretty awkward since, from what I can gather, we aren't going to buy the restaurant space."

Dana looked to Hayes. "Is that what you and your brothers have decided?"

"We're still discussing it." That wasn't quite true but he really didn't want to get into this right now. If he couldn't talk his brother out of this, then he'd contact the rest of the guys and let them deal with it. His job had been to come up here and check out the situation and if at all possible, put an end to it.

"Why don't you take McKenzie for a horseback ride?" Dana suggested to Hayes. "It's beautiful up in the mountains behind the ranch and it will take both of your minds off your problems."

He was glad for anything that let him escape more discussion about the restaurant, so he jumped at it. "Good idea."

He found McKenzie standing outside on the wide Western porch, leaning on the porch railing and looking toward the mountains beyond. At his approach, she turned to smile at him.

"Thank you," she said, turning to him. She'd changed out of the suit she'd been wearing earlier into jeans and blouse. "This place is beautiful. I feel…safe here and I adore your cousin Dana."

"Everyone does. I thought you'd like it here. That

was the plan. Dana suggested a horseback ride up into the mountains. What do you say?"

"Really? I'd love to." She sounded so excited he couldn't help but smile. He was reminded again of that moment last night when he'd looked into her eyes and felt…something.

"Great. Dana said she has two gentle horses that should be perfect for us greenhorns."

"Speak for yourself," McKenzie said. "I grew up riding and I suspect you did, too," she said, eyeing him. "Or is that Stetson and those boots just for show?"

He laughed. "I've ridden a few horses in my day."

Dana came out of the house then with a pair of boots she thought would fit McKenzie. They all visited as she led them up to the corral and got them saddled up for their ride.

Hayes noticed that McKenzie's step was lighter. He felt uncomfortable playing hero protector, but he preferred that to worrying about her. He'd learned as a private investigator to follow his own instincts. If she felt she was being watched, he knew there was the chance she probably was.

Chapter Six

He couldn't believe his good luck at finding McKenzie Sheldon's face on that real-estate sign. He took this as an omen that things were going to work out, after all.

Whistling all the way back to his house, he planned his new strategy. From the description the newspaper had run of the attacker, he felt assured that McKenzie hadn't gotten a good look at him. Which meant she wouldn't know him if she saw him again. But he had to be sure before he moved forward.

He checked the real-estate listings and found an open house she was hosting on Sunday, day after tomorrow. But to his delight, he saw that she was going to be the featured speaker at a real-estate conference being held at the university right here in town tomorrow.

He imagined that she was scared after last night. He just hoped she didn't cancel her speech or her open house or have someone else host it. Given the fight she'd put up last night, he had a feeling she wouldn't. He liked that about her and couldn't wait to see her again.

Excited now and much relieved, he felt better than he

had since his failure the night before. But he wouldn't be satisfied until he fixed this.

From as far back as he could remember, he couldn't bear failing. He supposed that was his parents' fault. They'd expected so much of him—too much. He would have given anything to make them happy, and he'd certainly tried for years. But he'd only disappointed them time and time again.

The thought left a bitter taste in his mouth.

His parents weren't the only ones. He'd also disappointed his girlfriends. The thought of them made his stomach roil. He'd never known what they wanted from him. It was this secret that women kept among themselves. They would get that self-satisfied smirk on their faces, mocking you for failing.

"I should have expected as much from you," his high school girlfriend used to say. And when he begged her to just tell him what she wanted, she would add, "If you don't know, then there is really nothing more I can say."

The bitches had played their games with him throughout high school and then college. He'd tried to understand them. Even with his longest relationship after college, four years, he'd continued to disappoint. Nothing was ever good enough. And the nagging...

That was really when things had started to change. After his breakup following four years of torture, he'd picked up a woman at the bar and taken her for a ride out into the country. All he'd wanted was sex and a little peace and quiet. But it had proven too much to ask. She'd started going off on him, about how she should have known at the bar that he was a loser. He'd told her to get out of his car.

"Out here? No, you take me back to the bar where I left my car right now," she'd said.

He remembered looking at her. How ugly women were when they scowled like that. "Get out of my car right now or I am going to kill you."

She'd started to argue, but something in his expression had stopped her. She got out and began to cry, yelling obscenities as he backed up to leave. "I'm going to tell on you! Everyone is going to know about you!"

He'd hit the brakes, then threw the car into first gear and hit the gas as she began to run. That had shut her up. He'd chased her down the road until she'd had the sense to run into the trees. He'd been so calm as he'd turned off the car and gone into the trees after her.

She'd been easy to catch.

That was when he'd officially quit trying to please other people. Now he only worried about making himself happy. And what would make him happy was finding McKenzie Sheldon and finishing what he'd started.

MCKENZIE SHIFTED IN her saddle as she stared across rows of mountaintops to the sunset. The waning sun had left streaks of pink, orange and gold that fanned up into Montana's big sky.

"It's breathtaking." She turned to look at Hayes. "Thank you for bringing me up here. You were right, your family is so inviting, especially Dana. This was so kind of her."

"She is one in a million, no doubt about that."

"You all seem so close. My family is spread out all over the place. I only have one sister here in town and I don't see her much. My fault. I work all the time." She let out a sigh.

"I never met the Cardwell side of my family until this trip," Hayes said. "My mother left my father when us boys were very young and took us to Texas to live. We only saw our father on occasion, so this is my first time in Montana—and meeting my cousin Dana."

McKenzie couldn't help being surprised. "You seem so at home here."

He chuckled at that. "Montana does that to a person. Look at my brother. He intends to stay, restaurant or no restaurant."

"You're opposed to opening a Texas Boys Barbecue here?"

"It's complicated."

"I'm sorry, I shouldn't have asked." She looked toward the sunset and breathed in the sweet scent of the tall pines around her.

"No, it's fine. It's just that we started small, in an old house in Houston, and the business just…mushroomed. My brother Laramie has a head for that end of it and runs the corporation so the rest of us can pursue other careers."

"I understand you're a private investigator in Houston?"

He nodded. "Maybe it's just me, but our little barbecue joint has grown into something I never wanted it to be. Adding another one in Montana… Well, it was never in the plans. We swore we would at least keep them all in Texas."

She said nothing, hating that she had a dog in the fight. This was something the brothers would have to sort out among themselves. Meanwhile, she feared Tag would lose the restaurant space and clearly he had his heart set on his own business in Big Sky.

"It makes it all the more difficult because there are five of us," Hayes said. "Do you come from a large family?"

She laughed. "Nine children."

His eyes widened in surprise. "Imagine all of them having to agree on something."

"Impossible."

Hayes nodded, but he looked upset by the situation.

"Your brother is still going to marry the woman he loves and stay in Montana no matter what happens with the restaurant, right?"

"Seems so. I just hate to disappoint him, but it isn't as if he needs a job."

"Some people just enjoy working," she said, realizing how true that was. She couldn't imagine retiring, say, ten years from now even though she probably could. What would she do all day if she did?

"I suppose we should head back," Hayes said as the sky around them began to darken. The breeze stirred the thick pine boughs and McKenzie felt a chill, even though the day was still warm. "Sorry to dump my problems on you."

"Yes, I have more than enough of my own," she

joked. "Seriously, it was nice to think about someone else's for a while."

"I'm glad you're staying here on the ranch. Dana has invited us for a cookout tonight. You'll get to meet the rest of the family."

"I don't know how I will ever be able to repay her," McKenzie said.

"Just being here makes her happy since I think she gets starved for female companionship with all thesc Cardwell men around."

As they rode back toward the ranch, she couldn't help but notice the pines shimmering in the waning light. In the distance, she could see Lone Mountain, now a deep purple.

She couldn't remember a time she'd enjoyed a man's company the way she did Hayes Cardwell's. He wasn't hard to look at, either, she thought with a hidden smile, surprising herself. No man had turned her head in a very long time. And he really had taken her mind off last night.

But as they rode into the darkening ranch yard, she felt another shiver and tried to shake off that feeling of being watching again.

HAYES NOTICED HOW quiet McKenzie was at supper. Fortunately, his father and uncle hadn't been able to make it to the ranch so she'd only had to meet a few of the family members. He could tell she was exhausted. The ride, though, had put some color back into her cheeks.

After dinner, the two of them headed for their respective cabins on the mountainside behind the house and he asked, "Would it be possible for you to take a few days off? I'm anxious to have a look around the area and thought you might want to come along."

He could see that she saw through his ruse right away.

She smiled politely, though, and said, "I am speaking at a real-estate convention tomorrow at the university before several hundred people."

That had been his fear. "You can't get someone else to do it for you?"

"Are you kidding?" She laughed. "This has been planned for months."

He nodded. "So it's been widely publicized."

She frowned. "You can't think that the man who attacked me would come to something like this, hoping to harm me."

He wasn't sure what to think. "I don't like it because it will be hard to protect you in a crowd like that."

"Hayes—"

"If you're going to tell me that you don't want my protection, save your breath. I'm going with you."

"You'll be bored to tears."

"I hope so. I'm sure your speech will knock 'em dead, but with any luck, it will be uneventful."

"This conference is important. It's about growth in Montana, especially in this Big Sky area," she said as they neared her cabin.

Moonlight filled the canyon, casting long shadows from the pines. A breeze stirred the boughs, sending the sweet scent of pine into the night air. Overhead stars glittered above the canyon walls.

McKenzie met his gaze and smiled. "Good for *both* of our businesses, actually. There's a lot of money that has moved into Montana. A Texas barbecue restaurant at Big Sky wouldn't have made it maybe even five years ago. Now, though?" She raised an eyebrow.

"I know you aren't just saying that to sell the building we looked at."

"That building would already be sold if your brother hadn't put down money on it," she said.

Hayes's brow shot up. "Tag put money down on it?"

She realized she'd let the cat out of the bag. "I'm sorry, I got the impression it was his own money and merely to hold it until you could all see it."

"I knew he had his heart set on this, but..." He shook his head as they reached her cabin.

A small lantern-shaped light cast a golden glow from the porch over them and the wooden lattice swing that moved restlessly in the light breeze. Dana and Hud had the half-dozen guest cabins built to look as if they'd been there for a hundred years. They were rustic on the outside but had all the conveniences of home inside.

"I hope you and you brothers can work this out," McKenzie said.

"Me, too."

"Thank you again for everything," she said as she looked past him toward the old two-story ranch house below. "I've loved getting to know some of your family and the horseback ride... Well, I can't tell you how much I needed it, needed all of this."

"You know, Dana said you are welcome to stay as long as you want."

She smiled at that. “That is very sweet of her, but with Tag’s wedding just weeks away… No, I need to get back to work.”

“I understand. What time is this conference tomorrow?”

McKenzie told him and reluctantly agreed to his following her to her condo and then to the university.

“I hope you didn’t think I was trying to strong-arm you into the restaurant site,” she said.

He shook his head. “I didn’t. McKenzie, I was thinking we should have dinner some night before I return to Texas.”

“I would enjoy that.”

He waited for her to enter the cabin and turn on a light before he started through the pines to his own cabin. As he walked, he pulled out his cell phone and called his brother Laramie. It was such a beautiful June night and he wasn’t tired at all. If anything, he didn’t want the night to end. He couldn’t remember being this…

For a moment, he didn’t recognize the emotion. Happy. He laughed to himself. He felt…happy.

“Tag has his heart set on opening a restaurant here,” he said without preamble when his brother Laramie answered.

“We already knew that. What did you think about the location he picked?”

“What is the point of discussing that if we don’t want to open one in Montana?” he demanded. “Wait a minute. He called you, didn’t he?”

Laramie sighed. “He wanted to make sure I was flying in for the wedding in a few weeks so I could see the site and we could talk. You didn't tell him what we decided, I take it? Is this just a case of you not wanting to play the bad guy?"

"No, I'm actually reconsidering." Hayes told himself it had nothing to do with McKenzie Sheldon and much more to do with Montana. He was falling for the state. He wouldn't be here long enough to fall for the woman, which was another reason not to stay too long. Fate might have thrown them together, but then again, he didn't believe in fate, did he? "Tag made some good points."

"So would the location work?"

"The location is fine. Actually better than fine. And maybe Big Sky is ready for Texas barbecue, but is this really something we want to do? What's next, Wyoming? Minnesota?"

"Tag said that people from all over the world visit Big Sky and a lot of the homeowners have sophisticated tastes."

Hayes laughed. "You aren't really implying that our barbecue requires a sophisticated taste."

"Maybe not, but our beans definitely do."

They both laughed.

"So tell me about his fiancée," Laramie said.

"She's pretty, supersmart, has a great job and owns her own home here in Big Sky. And she's definitely wild about our brother."

"Sounds like our Tag hit a home run."

Hayes sighed. "She's nice, too. I liked her."

"I heard you found a woman up there, as well."

"*Found* being the operative word." Hayes told his brother what had happened.

"Crazy. I thought there wasn't any crime up there."

"Low crime. Not *no* crime." He'd reached his cabin. As he climbed up the steps and sat down on the porch swing, he said, "I'm thinking I might stick around for a while." It surprised him that he'd voiced what had been in the back of his mind.

"So it's like that," Laramie said.

"It's…complicated."

"Be careful, Hayes," his brother warned. "You know what Jackson went through with his marriage."

He did. His wife had left him right after their son was born, only to come back three years later and try to take Ford away from Jackson. "Could you fly up now instead of before the wedding?"

"Not going to happen. Let's remember that I'm the brother who keeps Texas Boys Barbecue Corporation going."

"We never forget that," Hayes said. Laramie was the business major, the brother who'd gladly taken the reins when the business had begun to take off. True, it had grown more than any of them had anticipated since then, but Laramie was still the best brother to be in charge. And there was that added benefit that none of them forgot. Laramie allowed the rest of them to do whatever they wanted, never having to worry about money.

"You know how thankful we all are that you took it on," he said, not that Laramie needed reassurance. His brother loved what he did and continued to make the corporation more than profitable.

"What about Austin?" Hayes had to ask.

Silence, then Laramie said in a worried tone, "He's on a case down by the border. I haven't been able to reach him for several weeks now."

Hayes let out a curse. When Austin got on a case, it was all-consuming. They often went for weeks, even months, with no word from him. He only seemed to take on the most dangerous cases. They'd almost lost him more than once.

"I thought he was working fewer hours for the sheriff's department."

"You know him better than that," Laramie said. "I'm sure he will do everything possible to make the wedding, though."

Hayes sure hoped so, but of the five of them, Austin was the loner of the family and possibly the most stubborn. "When are Jackson and Ford flying in?" He knew Jackson and his five-year-old son wouldn't miss the wedding, even though weddings were the last thing Jackson was interested in attending after his marriage had gone so awry.

"A few days before the wedding. Ford is excited about riding horses at the ranch. Apparently, cousin Dana promised him his own horse while he's up there."

"So what do you want me to do about Tag and the restaurant site?" Hayes asked.

"If you've already weakened, I'd say it was a done deal."

As Hayes disconnected, he thought about walking

back to McKenzie's cabin and telling her to get the paperwork for the restaurant site ready. It was pretty much a done deal if Laramie was getting behind it.

But he stayed on his cabin porch. He could tell her tomorrow or maybe even the next day. It would give him an excuse to see her again. Not that he needed one. What was that old Chinese proverb? *He who saves a life is responsible for it.*

The woman brought out his protective instincts. He knew it was because she was so strong, so determined, so capable of taking care of herself under normal circumstances. But the man who'd attacked her had shaken her world and left her afraid and vulnerable.

Hayes told himself that whoever had tried to abduct her in the grocery-store parking lot was probably long gone.

But what if he wasn't? What if it was this man she'd fired?

He swore softly under his breath. It seemed that tomorrow he was going to a huge real-estate conference where a predator could be anyone in the crowd. And to think he'd actually considered leaving his gun in Texas, asking himself, *what were the chances he would need it in Montana?*

Chapter Seven

The moment they reached what McKenzie called the "field house," a huge, circular, dome-shaped building on the Montana State University campus, Hayes saw the parking lot and knew this was going to be a security nightmare.

As they entered the building, they were surrounded by people, many of them coming up to McKenzie. There were pats on the back, handshakes, people brushing her arm in welcome as she made her way down to the exhibits.

"Are you all right?" McKenzie asked when they finally got to M.K. Realty's booth.

"It's not me I'm worried about."

"You've been scowling since we got here," she said. "Haven't you ever heard of safety in numbers?"

She seemed to be at ease, as if she'd forgotten the attack, but Hayes wasn't fooled. He could see past the bravado. She was putting on a show, determined that her attacker wasn't going to change anything about her life.

But he already had. She either was pretending otherwise or the reality of it hadn't hit home yet.

"Sorry," he said. "I'll try to lighten up. Or at least look as if I have."

She gave him a grateful smile and squeezed his arm. "I really do appreciate that you're here."

Let's see if you do when this day is over, he thought, wondering how he was going to keep her safe in a place this packed with people.

As she had a word with her employees at their booth, he watched the crowd. He had some idea of who he was looking for. A large man, over six feet, strongly built.

He'd had a few cases involving these types of men. While he knew the general type, there were always exceptions. He wasn't going to make the mistake of trying to pigeonhole this one.

The place was filled with men, most of them alone. Any one of these men could be here to hurt McKenzie. The thought rattled him so much that he didn't hear her saying his name. When she touched his arm, he jumped.

She gave him a pleading look. She was trying so hard to hold it together. She didn't need him wigging out on her.

"He could be miles from here," she whispered as she stepped close. He felt her breath on his ear and shivered inwardly. Just the light scent of her perfume had his pulse thrumming.

Today she'd worn a business suit with a white blouse under the jacket that accentuated her olive skin and the thin silver necklace around her neck. At the end of the chain, a small diamond rested between the swell of her breasts. She'd put makeup on the bruises at her neck, hiding them enough that no one would notice. Diamond studs glittered on each of her earlobes with her hair pulled up off her long, slim neck.

She'd chosen a shade of lipstick that called attention to her full mouth. No way could this woman possibly blend into this crowd.

"Are you listening to me?" she asked.

He nodded, although his thoughts had been on the way the suit skirt hugged her shapely behind, dropping below her knees to her long legs and the matching high heels on her feet. McKenzie was the whole package. Any man in his right mind would want this woman.

As it was, somewhere in this building could be a man completely out of his mind who, if he got the chance, would hurt her and bury her in a shallow grave somewhere.

"Why don't you stay here? You'll be able to see me from here." She pointed to a raised area where she would be giving her speech.

Before he could object, she took off through the crowd. He went after her, fighting his way through the throng of people. He caught a glimpse of her head as she neared the platform and knew he wouldn't be able to catch up to her before she was on stage.

MCKENZIE COULDN'T HELP being irritated with Hayes. She needed his strength right now. Seeing the worry in his eyes only made her more aware of what had happened to her two nights ago.

But she'd put it behind her, convinced the man had been traveling through town and was now miles from here.

She cut through the crowd, not stopping even to say

hello to people she knew. She was in the people business. It really did matter who you knew when you sold real estate, she was thinking as she neared the side of the raised platform and the podium and microphone waiting for her.

Rows of chairs had been placed in front and were already full. She'd been honored when asked to speak. Some of the older Realtors resented her because she'd climbed so fast.

She thought of Gus Thompson's mother. She'd been McKenzie's mentor and had taught her the ropes.

"Of course they don't like it," she'd said once when McKenzie had mentioned that some of the Realtors had given her the cold shoulder. "Just keep your chin up and don't lose sight of where it is you want to go."

It had been good advice. She hadn't made enemies along the way and was glad of that. Instead, she'd kept her nose to the grindstone, working hard and now knew she had the respect of her peers. Several of the older Realtors gave her a nod as she passed.

She made her way to the stairs at the back of the platform near the wall and had started up the stairs when her hair was grabbed from behind. Her head jerked back. She heard the sound of something sharp cutting through her hair an instant before the pressure on it was released.

Fighting to keep from falling back down the couple of stairs she'd climbed, she swung around, thinking she must have caught her hair on something.

There were people everywhere but none were paying

any attention to her. Nor could she see anything that might have caught in her hair.

Her hand went to her long, blond mane. In the middle of the back of her head she felt a place where a huge chunk of her hair had been chopped off only inches from her scalp.

She looked down to see a few long strands on the stairs along with the clip she'd used to put her hair up this morning.

Her body began to shake. Someone had grabbed her from behind and chopped off a huge chunk of her hair? It was inconceivable. But then so was what had happened to her the night in the grocery-store parking lot.

On the stage, one of the Realtors was checking the microphone as she got ready to announce the guest speaker.

McKenzie looked again at the people milling past. No one seemed to pay her any mind. No one had a hank of her hair in his hand. But she knew it could have been any one of them.

She quickly stepped back down the stairs to retrieve her clip. Her fingers trembled as she pulled her hair up as best she could and anchored it with the clip.

She could do this. She would do this. She wouldn't be scared off. She wouldn't let whoever had done this win.

SOMETHING WAS WRONG. Hayes watched McKenzie walk onto the stage smiling. But he knew her smile and that wasn't it.

His heart began to pound. He shouldn't have let her out of his sight. The darn woman. She was so stubborn, so sure she could handle this on her own. She hadn't been out of his sight for more than a few moments—not until she'd gone behind the raised platform.

Whatever had happened must have occurred there. But with so many people around…

He watched her walk up to the microphone. He could see her trying to pull herself together. She looked down at her notes. Even from a distance he thought he saw her hands trembling.

She laid her notes down on the podium and leaned toward the microphone. Her voice was clear and true as she looked up at the crowd gathered to hear her speak.

Hayes had admired her, but right now he was in awe of her courage and fortitude. He could practically see the determination in her shoulders, in her voice, in those amazing eyes of hers. She stood there and gave her speech with probably more spirit than she would have if something hadn't happened before she'd stepped up to that microphone.

She was beautiful, a woman to be reckoned with, and Hayes knew he wasn't the only man in the audience who thought so.

When she finished, she was met with applause and even a standing ovation.

She beamed, raising her chin into the air, her eyes bright. The look on her face filling him with fear.

If the man who'd attacked her was somewhere in that crowd watching her, McKenzie was letting him know she wasn't scared of him and that she was far from defeated.

It was the kind of challenge that would only antagonize her attacker—and get her killed.

HAYES WAS WAITING for her as she descended the stairs behind the platform. She saw his expression and had to look away to keep from breaking down. He knew. How, she had no idea.

He took her arm without a word and led her toward the closest exit. She kept a smile on her face, nodding to people she knew. Hayes didn't slow down until he had her out the door and almost to his rental car.

"What happened?" he asked the moment he had her safely in the passenger seat with him behind the wheel.

She reached up and unclipped her hair. It fell past her shoulders except for the part that had been whacked off. She put down the car's visor mirror and got her first look at the damage that had been done.

Hayes let out a curse.

The savagery of the act more than the loss of the hair brought tears to her eyes. "It will grow back. It's just hair."

He let out another oath. "He's telling you that he's not done with you. He's telling you—"

"I know what he's telling me," she snapped as she turned to face him. "It's just hair. He won't get that close to me again."

Hayes pulled off his Stetson and raked a hand through his own hair as if he was too angry to speak.

"You can't give him another chance at you," he said after a moment. "Today? It was too dangerous. You need to cancel your appointments until the police find this guy."

"What I need is a haircut."

His expression softened as he met her gaze. He must have seen how close she was to tears and how badly she was fighting not to cry. "Where do you want me to take you?"

"A friend of mine owns a salon. I'm sure under the circumstances she will be able to squeeze me in."

"After that, we need to talk," he said as he started the car and pulled out of the lot, wondering if her attacker was watching them drive away.

HE PUT THE fistful of McKenzie Sheldon's hair to his nose and smelled the sweet scent. She'd probably shampooed it this morning in the shower. He let himself imagine her standing under the warm spray for a moment. He would never see her like that, arms raised as she gently worked the shampoo into her long, blond hair.

Rubbing the hair between his fingers, he studied it in the light of the men's room. It was hard to know the exact color. Pale summer sun, he thought. Too bad he couldn't show the hair to someone who would know what to call it.

He would keep the hair. Maybe he would tie a ribbon around it. Not even an hour ago, it had been growing on her head. That thought stirred the need within. He ached with it and wasn't sure how much longer he could go without fulfilling it.

Someone came into the men's room. He put the hair

into the pocket of his jacket, careful not to let any of it escape. He'd lost some of the strands on the stairs as it was. He didn't want to lose any more.

The idea of cutting her hair hadn't even crossed his mind until he'd grabbed hold of it as she'd started up those stairs. He'd wanted her to stumble. Maybe even fall. He had needed to know if she would recognize him when she saw him. The idea of her falling into his arms was just too mouthwatering to pass up.

He'd told himself that just touching her again would be enough. But then she'd gone behind that platform out of sight of the cowboy she'd come with, the same one, he suspected, who'd saved her at the grocery-store parking lot.

Seeing his chance, he'd grabbed her hair, felt its silky smoothness… He always had his scissors with him, sharpened to a lethal edge. When he'd grabbed her hair, felt it in the fingers of his right hand, his left had gone for the scissors.

At that moment, he'd wanted a piece of her—since that was all he was going to get until he could catch her alone.

Now, feeling better than he had since the night he'd failed, he left the bathroom one hand deep in the pocket of his jacket where he kept the scissors, the other gently caressing her hair. It was enough for today, he thought, anxious to get out of the building so he could be alone.

Soon, McKenzie Sheldon. Very soon and it will be more than your hair that I have my hands on.

"ARE YOU SURE you don't want me to take your open

house today?" Jennifer Robinson asked when McKenzie called the office.

"No, I can handle it, but thanks, Jennifer." She wasn't looking forward to the open house. Someone had tried to scare her yesterday.

Now she looked at her short curly hair in the mirror. Hayes had complimented her hairdo when she'd come out of the salon. "It looks good on you."

She'd always hated her natural curly hair, brushing it straight every morning after her shower. It felt odd, the loss of weight she'd become used to. She raked her hand through the curls and told herself she liked it better short—a lie, one she told herself every time she remembered the sudden feel of her head being pulled back, then the sound of something sharp cutting through her long hair before her head snapped forward again.

It had happened so fast.

And could again, Hayes had reminded her. She knew he was angry with her for taking off yesterday without him with her—and for not hiding out. He didn't want her hosting this open house today. He didn't understand. She couldn't hide. She refused to let this man take away everything she'd worked so hard for.

"At least come back to the ranch tonight," Hayes had pleaded yesterday after the conference. "I can keep you safe there."

She'd been scared and shaken enough that she'd agreed to go back up the canyon to Cardwell Ranch rather than return to her condo. Her evening had been so relaxing and enjoyable she'd never wanted to leave. Dana's husband, Marshal Hud Savage, had cooked steaks outside on the grill and they'd all eaten on the wide porch to enjoy the beautiful night.

She'd been completely captivated by the Cardwells, especially Hayes. He had an easygoing way about him that appealed to her. It amazed her that she'd thought there was anything threatening about him. It was his eyes. She'd remembered them from the night of the attack. They had been comforting. Just like his words. *You're safe now.*

Only she wasn't.

She reminded herself of that as she drove from Big Sky into Bozeman, determined to get on with her life.

"At least let me take you to your open house," he'd argued.

"You can't be with me 24/7 and I refuse to hide under a rock. He's trying to scare me."

"Until he tries to abduct you again and kill you. McKenzie, he knows who you are."

His last words had sent an icy chill through her. *He knows who you are.*

But she didn't know who he was. He could have been anyone in that crowd yesterday.

Angry with herself for letting her thoughts take that turn, she told herself she would put the attack behind her. Big words, she thought as she drove up in front of her condo and just sat there, engine running, surprised how hard it was to face going inside. She knew it was crazy. The attack hadn't even happened here. And yet she had the crazy fear that he would be inside, waiting for her….

Getting out of her SUV, she gripped her keys as she made her way to the front door. She noticed her neighbor had already gone to work. A quiet had settled over the four units. She'd picked this condo because of all the pine trees and the creek that meandered past it.

Now, though, the thick pines made her nervous and the babbling stream quickly put her nerves on edge. She got the key into the lock and pushed open the door.

She wasn't sure what she'd expected to find. Maybe the place ransacked. Everything looked exactly as she'd left it. She stepped in. An eerie silence settled around her. She'd always loved coming home. The condo had been decorated simply with light colors that made the rooms feel welcoming. She'd always felt at peace here.

Now, however, she opened her shoulder bag and took out the pepper spray she'd bought yesterday. Holding it, she moved quickly through the two-story condo, checking closets and bathrooms and even under beds until she was sure she was alone.

She was trembling more from fear than from the effort of searching the spacious condo. The fear made her angry with herself. She couldn't keep living like this.

When her cell phone rang, she jumped. Stilling her heart, she took the call. It was her sister.

"How are you doing?" Shawna asked.

"Fine." The lie seemed to catch in her throat. "Not as well as I'd hoped."

"If you need company—"

"No, I'm keeping busy. I have an open house today."

"Work as usual, huh? That's my little sis. Well, if you need anything, you know to call."

"I will. Thank you."

As she hung up, she saw that Gus Thompson had left a message. She braced herself and played it.

"We need to talk. Call me."

Just the sound of his voice made her stomach ache. What did he think they needed to talk about? And why was he so insistent? She still couldn't believe he was the man who'd attacked her, but maybe she just didn't want to. She'd worked with him for years. Surely she would have known he was dangerous, wouldn't she?

McKenzie quickly showered and changed for her open house, determined not to let Gus or anyone else keep her from her work. She had a business to run. She had to go over everything she needed, afraid that as distracted as she was, she would forget something important. The open house needed to go off just right. This was a major sale for a contractor she liked working with, so she hoped to get an offer before the day was out.

Hurrying so she could get to the house early, she exited her front door and was just pulling the door closed after her when the man stepped out of the shadows.

HAYES SWUNG BY the restaurant site before heading to McKenzie's open house. He wanted to see the traffic flow in the area and take another look around. The other day, he'd been distracted and determined they weren't buying the space. But after talking to his brother Laramie, he'd tried to reach Austin. He'd been told that Austin was on a case and couldn't be reached. He couldn't help worrying about him.

He felt at loose ends. His attempt to talk McKenzie out of hosting the open house today had fallen on deaf ears. Did she really think that by pretending none of this was happening it would stop this bastard? All she had to do was look in the mirror to see just how close the man had gotten to her—again.

He'd been shocked last night after dinner when she'd told him about the open house, but he'd tried not to argue with her. He'd seen the way she could dig her heels in. Look at what had happened yesterday. Maybe his concern *had* put her in more danger. He was determined not to let that happen again.

"Can't someone else host it?" he'd suggested.

"I could get someone else to do it, but…I can't." She'd shrugged as if it was hard to explain.

"I get it," he'd said. "You're like my brother Laramie. We've offered to help with the load, but…"

"He has it handled."

"Yep, and he does a fine job of it. I noticed that you own your realty company." She was young to have accomplished so much so quickly. He wondered if she'd had help and decided not. It was that tenacity about her that intrigued him. But also frustrated him because her determination not to let her attacker interfere with her life put her in danger.

"It was a lot of hard work, but when you want something badly enough…" Her voice had dropped off and he'd realized she was thinking about the man she'd fought off repeatedly the night of her attack. Neither would have given up. If Hayes hadn't come out of the store when he had…

"What kind of open house is it?" he'd asked to derail her thoughts—and his own.

"A brand-new, state-of-the-art, spacious, three-thousand-square-foot executive home overlooking Bozeman with beautiful views of the Spanish Peaks."

He'd laughed and she'd joined him. He was glad she could laugh at herself.

"I did sound like a Realtor, didn't I?" She sighed. "Bad habit."

"Let me guess. All restaurant-quality appliances and granite countertops in the massive kitchen. I had the flu recently and found myself watching some of those home shows on television. Talk about over the top."

She'd nodded in agreement. "You do see a lot of… extravagance in some of the homes in this area, too. Gold faucets, heated driveways, dual master suites."

"You love what you do," he'd said as if he'd just seen it.

She'd smiled, tears in her eyes. "That's why I can't let him stop me."

"Or me stop you," he'd said, and she'd nodded before she'd leaned over and gently placed a kiss on his cheek.

Their eyes met and locked and for one breath-stealing moment he'd almost taken her in his arms, even though he knew he wanted a lot more than a kiss. Fortunately, or unfortunately, they'd been interrupted by the kids running in to say good-night as they headed to bed.

The moment had been lost, filling him with regret and relief at the same time. His life was in Houston. He reminded himself of that now.

Determined to get at least the barbecue joint settled, he called Jackson. Ford answered the phone. The five-year-old sounded so grown-up. Hayes tried to remember the last time he'd seen his nephew. It had been too long, that was for sure.

"Hey, kid," he said. "What have you been up to?"

Ford was a chatterbox on the phone. Hayes listened to stories about sports, the trouble his nephew had gotten into and how they would be flying to Montana for his uncle Tag's wedding to some girl before Ford launched into an excited story about the horse Dana had picked out for him to ride once he got to Montana.

Finally, Hayes had to ask if he could speak to the boy's father.

Jackson came on the line.

"How much of that can I believe?" Hayes joked.

His brother laughed. "Ford's into Texas tall tales I'm afraid, just like his uncles. What's this I hear about Laramie supporting the Montana restaurant?"

"I talked to him last night. Tag's convinced him. I have to admit, I've weakened, as well."

"What about this future bride?"

Hayes could hear the concern in Jackson's voice. He'd gotten burned badly. He didn't want to see his brother Tag go through a divorce.

"She's nice. I liked her. She's got plenty of her own money, a good job, a nice house up on the mountain behind Big Sky. Clearly, they are crazy about each other."

Jackson snorted. He knew crazy.

"I'm standing in front of the restaurant space right now. I think we should move ahead with this."

Jackson sounded surprised. "What changed your mind?"

"I actually think it's a good business decision. Also, I guess I want to do this for Tag."

"Is everyone else in agreement?"

"Can't reach Austin. Nothing new there." But he figured Austin would go along with whatever was decided. He had little interest in the business, too involved in being a sheriff's deputy and saving the world.

"As long as Tag's new wife isn't involved in the business in any way, I'm good with it," Jackson said. "I still have time to meet her and see what I think before he can get the place open."

No one was more cynical than Jackson.

"I think this is the right thing to do," Hayes said, checking his watch. "I'll tell the Realtor when I see her."

GUS WAS GLAD he'd scared her. He took enjoyment in McKenzie's shock and fear. How did she think he felt being interrogated by the police and suddenly out of a job?

"Gus." She said his name on a frightened breath, her hand going to her chest as she stumbled back against her closed condo door.

He'd seen her lock it so he knew she wasn't going to be able to get back inside away from him until he had his say. He closed the distance, forcing her up against the door, towering over her. She'd cut her hair. It surprised him. He'd always thought she liked it long. He wondered what had precipitated this? Out with the old, in with the new? Had she already replaced him at the agency?

"What do you want?" Her voice actually squeaked. Where was that ball-breaking woman he'd worked for the past six years?

"What do I *want?*" he repeated. "I want to know why you're ruining my life."

Some of her steel returned to her voice. "This isn't the place to talk about this."

He laughed. "Where would that place be, McKenzie? You've taken out a restraining order against me so I can't go near the office or you."

Some of the color came back into her face. "It should be obvious why I had to do that."

"Because you think I'm some kind of psycho? Do you really think I attacked you in a grocery parking lot?"

"I don't know. Were you at the conference yesterday?"

"Why? Were you attacked again?" He smirked. "Do you really think I can show my face at a real-estate conference right now?"

He could tell she didn't believe him. "I thought I saw you there."

"Well, you were wrong. The same way you were wrong to fire me."

"I'm sure I wasn't the first person you've stalked. You've been harassing my receptionist. I told you that if I had to warn you again..."

He looked at her in disbelief. "Maybe I was *interested* in you, did you ever consider that? I came by your house that day to ask you out, but about the time I finally got up my nerve, you saw me. Your expression... Well, let's just say I knew my answer."

The woman he'd known was back. Anger flared in her eyes. She moved away from the door, forcing him to take a step back. "It's too bad you didn't take no from Cynthia."

He felt off-balance, something she'd made him feel way too many times. "I don't expect you to believe this, but she led me on. She liked me flirting with her."

"Up to a point, I'm sure that was true."

"And yet you fired *me*."

"It was a combination of things, Gus, not just a couple of incidents and you know it. You've always resented working for me."

He nodded, finally seeing it. His own anger boiled to the surface. "You were just waiting for my mother to die so you could get rid of me. As long as she was alive, you wouldn't dare."

"That isn't true." McKenzie looked at her watch, dismissing him. The old McKenzie Sheldon, businesswoman, had come back. "You're going to make me late for an open house and there really is no point to this discussion. I'm not changing my mind. If you promise to leave me alone in the future, I will write you a recommendation, not that you need one. You're a great salesman. Just stop trying to sell yourself to women who aren't in the market."

"That's it?"

"You brought this on yourself, Gus." She slipped past him.

He had no choice but to let her go. As he watched her drive away, he felt as if she'd punched him in the gut. He knew the best thing he could do was leave her alone, take the recommendation and start looking for another job.

But this still felt unfinished to him.

He stood outside the open house for a moment, wondering who could afford such a home—and what the commission would net McKenzie Sheldon. Probably more money than he made in months. He would never admit that that alone made him want to hurt this woman. The woman was obviously very successful. It would seem small of him to want to destroy her simply out of jealousy.

But a part of him had to admit, he liked to target successful women. He liked bringing them down. He smiled to himself, thinking how many of them he had made beg for their lives. They weren't so arrogant and sure of themselves then.

People were coming in and out of the open house. Beautiful June days probably brought more people out than stormy, wintery ones, he thought. He waited and fell behind a group of five. Being a salesman at heart himself, he quickly sized them up. The elderly married couple looked serious about home buying. The two women behind them were just gawkers. The lone man who'd led the way looked like another Realtor.

Once inside, he cut away from the others. The elderly couple made a beeline for McKenzie and the flyer she was handing out. He only got a glimpse of her. The last thing he wanted to do was get caught staring at her.

His plan had worked beautifully. He would wait until there were a lot of other people going through the house so he blended in. But at some point, he would have to get close enough to McKenzie Sheldon so he could look into her eyes and find out whether or not she recognized him.

Even a hint of recognition and he would get out of there. The best plan was to park a few blocks away and walk. Not that he expected her to chase him out to his car. Or even scream.

The house was no surprise. Every room was large and over the top with expensive features and furnishings. He wandered around, saw the older couple inspecting the fixtures and heard the two women oohing and ahhing over the kitchen.

As spacious as the house was, he felt claustrophobic and knew he couldn't take much more of this. He was working up his nerve to return to the main entrance and get one of the brochures from Ms. Sheldon, when he came around a corner and almost collided with her.

She pretended the encounter hadn't startled her, but he'd seen the terror flash in her eyes. Nice eyes, more green than blue today. Those eyes widened and for just a moment, he feared she'd recognized him. She was blocking the hallway and his way out. A fissure of panic raced along his nerve endings. Perspiration dampened his shirt and hairline.

He told himself that if she opened her mouth, he'd hit her. There wasn't anyone else around. He'd punch her hard enough to knock her out and then he'd push her into one of the bedrooms and leave quickly. He balled up one fist and took a breath.

But she didn't scream. The flash of terror had only lasted an instant then she'd looked relieved and relaxed a little.

"Sorry," she said. "You startled me."

Not as much as I did a few nights ago. He looked

right into those aquamarine waters. Not even a hint of recognition. He almost laughed since just an instant before he'd been planning to knock her senseless and make his escape.

"I'm sorry," he said. "We both must have been distracted."

"How do you like the house?" she asked, covering her initial reaction to him.

"It's beautiful." *Just like you.* She blew him away. She was much more striking than her photo on the real-estate signs. There was a sweetness about her. Strength? Oh, he knew her strength and her determination only too well. Sweet, strong and successful—his perfect woman.

"You might want one of these." She held out a flyer.

"Yes," he said and smiled. "Thank you. Oh, and do you have a business card?"

She brightened. "Of course. I usually have one stapled to the flyers. I forgot this morning. I have one in my purse if you'd like to follow me." She headed back toward the entrance. He followed her, admiring the part of her body he had some history with.

From under an entertainment counter, she pulled out her purse, removed a business card and handed it to him. The card was thick, nicely embossed. He rubbed it gently between his fingers. A business card told a lot about a person.

He carefully put it into his shirt pocket and folded the flyer she'd given him.

"Is there anything else I can help you with?" she asked.

"No, I think I have everything." He smiled. "But you'll be hearing from me."

McKenzie was just about to ask the man for his name when the front door opened and her attention was drawn away as she saw Hayes Cardwell come through the door.

A mixture of pleasure and relief filled her at the sight of the big cowboy. He wore jeans, a Western shirt and a gray Stetson over his longish dark hair. Unlike yesterday, he looked more relaxed.

Almost instinctively, she started to move toward him, but remembered the man who'd shown an interest in the house. She turned her attention back to him. "I look forward to hearing from you if you have any questions about the house or would like to see any others."

"Next time, I'd like to bring my wife along. I'll give you a call," the man said, glancing at Hayes before he quickly moved off.

McKenzie turned to Hayes. She always felt she had to be "on" at open houses. Even though she loved her job, sometimes it wasn't just her high-heeled shoes that made her hurt. Her face often ached from smiling so much.

"Decided you wanted a kitchen with all stainless-steel appliances and granite countertops?"

"Can't imagine living without them."

She chuckled at that. "You're saying you don't have them at your house in Houston?"

"I live in an unremodeled house in the older part of Houston."

She cocked an eyebrow at that.

"I have...humble tastes."

"Nothing wrong with that," she said. "Excuse me a moment." McKenzie saw a few more people she needed to talk to before they left. The elderly couple sounded interested. She gave them her business card. As she started to go look for Hayes, she saw the man she'd spoken to earlier before Hayes had come in.

The man was walking away when he suddenly stopped and turned to look back at her as if he'd known she'd be there framed in the front window, watching him. He gave a slow, vague kind of smile. She quickly stepped back out of sight, even though she feared he'd seen her. His smile had almost been mocking, as if he'd put one over on her.

She'd dealt with enough people at open houses that she had a pretty good sense of who was genuinely in the market for a house and who wasn't. The man had seemed interested and yet he hadn't asked any questions about the house—unlike the elderly couple. Maybe he *had* just been putting her on.

McKenzie went to find Hayes, annoyed with the man and herself. He might have fooled her once, but she would be watching for him at her next open house.

HAYES LOOKED AROUND the large residence, killing time until the open house was over. Several men came through. Any one of them could have been McKenzie's attacker.

At four o'clock, he found McKenzie finishing up with a couple and waited as she packed up to leave.

"Dinner. You name the restaurant," he said.

"I really should—"

"Work?" He saw her hesitate. "I figured since we both need to eat…"

She brushed a lock of hair back from her face. She'd dressed up for the open house, taking extra pains with her appearance. Probably to give herself more confidence. But under the surface, he would see that she was still running scared.

"Hayes, I appreciate what you're trying to do…."

"*Eat?* I like to do it three times a day, if possible."

"You know what I mean." She sighed. "You can't protect me forever, especially since you will be leaving soon."

He nodded. "So that must mean I'm just hungry, don't you think?"

She laughed. "Are you always so determined?"

"Always." He led the way out of the house and waited while she locked up. "By the way, how long do we have on that restaurant space at Big Sky?"

"Changed your mind?" she asked as they walked toward their vehicles.

"Tag isn't changing *his* mind." They'd reached his rented SUV. "Why don't you leave your car," he suggested. "I'll be happy to bring you back after dinner."

"Okay. Just let me put my things away."

He watched her put the flyers in the passenger seat and helped her place the Open House signs in the trunk. But as they finished, he noticed her look past him and frown. He turned but didn't see anything out of the ordinary.

"Is everything all right?" he asked.

"Hmm," she said distractedly. "Just someone I saw earlier at the open house. He must live in the neighborhood. It's nothing."

They ate a nice dinner, talked about everything but her attacker. Not that it kept the man from being present. Hayes doubted the attack was ever far from either of their minds.

He'd hoped McKenzie would be staying in the cabin at Cardwell Ranch, but she couldn't hide out, given her career. Not that a woman like her would let herself hide out forever, anyway, and the man might never be caught. Still, he didn't like the idea of McKenzie staying in her condo alone.

He'd told his brother he was staying until the wedding. It was only a few weeks away and if they were going ahead with the restaurant, he could help out. At least that was his excuse. In truth, he couldn't leave McKenzie. Not yet, even though she was right. He couldn't stay forever. Maybe it was best for her to start adjusting to living with never knowing when the man might reappear in her life.

"Dinner was wonderful," she said as they left the restaurant. "And a great idea."

"Thanks. I'm just full of great ideas," he said with a chuckle. "Like this one. I wish you would come back up to the ranch tonight."

She shook her head as he pulled up behind her car where they'd left it earlier for the open house. With the houses so far apart, the neighborhood was dark in the huge spaces between streetlamps. No lights burned in the house she'd shown earlier. With the houses bordered by tall, dense trees or high hedges, there were lots of places for a man to hide, he thought.

How many houses just like this did she show alone? He hated to think. In other places, he'd heard that real-estate agents now worked in twos to be safer. But this was Montana. People felt safe here.

"Thank you for the offer," she said. "I appreciate it, but I have a lot to do tomorrow."

He nodded, not surprised.

She opened her car door. "Have your brother give me a call about the restaurant space."

So that was how it was going to be? Business as usual? The woman was stubborn as a mule. She refused to take some time off, leave the state or at least town for a while. There was no way he could keep her safe and he couldn't just walk away.

He got out and caught up to her, catching her hand to turn her toward him. "I have a favor." She raised a brow. "I need a date for the wedding."

"Your brother's wedding?"

"Yes."

She shook her head. "I'm not your responsibility. I told you, you can't keep me safe."

"It's more complicated than that," he said as he touched her cheek. "From the moment I first looked in your eyes…" His words died off. She was staring at him. He shook his head. "Maybe I can't get you out of my mind—"

"I know what you're up to."

"I doubt that," he said, and leaned toward her, his hand looping around the back of her neck as he gently drew her to him. “Because if you could see what I was up to, then you’d know I was about to kiss you.”

He brushed his lips over hers, then pulled back to gaze into her eyes. He’d been captivated by those eyes two nights ago. That hadn’t changed. “Sorry, I couldn’t resist.”

“You don’t have to treat me as if I’m made out of glass and might break,” she said. “I’m a little battered right now, but I’m resilient and strong, a lot stronger than I look.”

“Is that right?” He looped an arm around her waist and pulled her to him right there in the street between their vehicles. He kissed her like he meant it this time. Her full lips parted in surprise. Her sweet, warm breath comingled with his own. She let out a soft moan as he tasted her. Drawing her even closer, he deepened the kiss, demanding more.

McKenzie came to him, fitting into his arms as she answered his kiss with passion. He felt desire race in a hot streak through his veins. He didn’t want to ever stop kissing her.

But when she pulled back, he let out a shaky breath. “Wow,” he said and laughed.

She sounded just as breathless. She met his gaze in the moonlight. “Hayes, what is this?”

“*This?* This is crazy. Worst possible timing ever.”

McKenzie nodded agreement.

“And yet, from the first moment I looked into your eyes…”

She shook her head. “I…I really can’t…. Hayes, I’m

not sure of anything right now and quite frankly, I'm suspicious of your motives."

"My motives for kissing you? It was just a kiss, right?"

She studied him openly in the dim light.

"Quite the kiss, though, wouldn't you say?" he asked, grinning.

She smiled at that. "Quite the kiss."

"Glad you agree. I'm still going to follow you home and make sure you're all right."

She looked as if she wanted to put up a fight, but no longer had the energy to. "Thank you," she said as she turned and started for her car. He watched her. She seemed a little wobbly on her high heels, strange for a woman who lived in them. He hoped the kiss had smacked her silly the way it had him. He'd kissed his share of women, but none had lit a fire in him the way McKenzie's kiss had.

As she reached the car, she hesitated. He saw her glance back at him, then reach for something on her windshield. His pulse leaped. Something was wrong. He was running toward her as she took what looked like a folded sheet of paper from under the wiper blade.

Chapter Eight

McKenzie had been shaken even before she found the note. The kiss had her whirling. It had been a while since a man had kissed her. She couldn't recall anyone who'd made her surrender so completely to a kiss before, though. She'd felt...*wanton,* and that wasn't a word she would have used about herself. She'd also felt out of control and that scared her.

Hayes had her blood running hot. He'd sparked something in her that made her ache for more. That alone was enough to turn her already crazy world upside down. She'd been content with her career, with her life, with an occasional date. Hayes had changed all that in just one kiss. Now she wanted...Hayes Cardwell. Bad timing or not.

But she questioned whether he was interested in her as a woman. Or if he was just hardwired to protect the woman whose life he'd saved because he was a Texas cowboy and a gentleman.

When she'd found the note under her windshield wiper, at first she'd thought it was an advertisement.

Instead, scrawled words had been written on the sheet of paper.

I'm watching you.
This time you won't get away.
I am going to miss your long hair.

The paper began to shake in her fingers. She had *felt* him watching her. It hadn't been her imagination. He was out there and he wasn't through with her.

She read the words again, all easily visible in the diffused light from the closest streetlamp. All her bravado fell away. The man wasn't giving up. He was out there. Maybe even watching her right now, wanting to see her fall apart.

McKenzie slumped against her car as she looked out into the darkness, unable to pretend any longer that she wasn't terrified. She'd thought she could go on as if nothing had happened. As if nothing kept happening.

Suddenly, Hayes was at her side, his arms coming around her. "What is it?" His gaze took in the sheet of paper trembling in her fingers. Using his sleeve, he took it from her. "Get in my car. I'll call the police."

She nodded and started for his rental SUV. Earlier, she'd told him how strong and resilient she was. She didn't feel either right now. She wanted to lose herself in his strong arms. For so long she'd made her way alone, determined not to lean on anyone, not to need anyone. Right now, she needed Hayes—and more than just to protect her.

Behind her, she heard him on the phone. Her gaze

swept through the dark neighborhood. A breeze stirred the tree boughs, throwing shadows everywhere. Was he out there watching her? Enjoying tormenting her?

McKenzie quickened her step, grabbed the passenger-side door handle and flung it open. She practically threw herself into the car, slamming the door behind her. Heart pounding, she tried to catch her breath. Anger mixed with fear, a deadly combination that had her wiping furiously at her tears.

She'd never felt helpless before. It was a horrible feeling, one she couldn't bear. Somehow, she had to make it end, and falling into bed with Hayes wasn't the answer as much as she would have liked to.

As Hayes finished his call and climbed into the SUV behind the wheel, she turned to him. "I have to find this man."

"I've called the police. They're on their way. They'll see if they can get a print off—"

"He won't have left fingerprints on the note he left for me. He's too smart for that." She shook her head. "Nor do I believe the police will find him. That's why I have to."

Hayes stared across the seat at her. "What are you saying?"

"I need to set a trap for him."

He held up a hand. "Hold on."

"No, I can't let him continue to torment me. I have to find him and put an end to this, one way or another."

HAYES DIDN'T KNOW how to tell her, but decided honesty might be the best approach. "I would imagine he will find you before you find him." He saw her reaction to his words. "He's fooling with you because you made a fool of him the other night. He has only one option. He needs to right this. Which means there's a really good chance that he isn't some psycho passing through town who just happened to see you the other night. He's a hometown psycho who isn't finished with you."

Her lower lip quivered for a moment before she bit down on it. "You sound as if you've dealt with this kind of...person before."

He nodded. "I've crossed paths with several. They're calculating, cunning and unpredictable—and extremely dangerous."

She leaned toward him and he was reminded of their kiss. He could smell her clean scent and remembered the feel of her in his arms. "Help me set a trap for him. I don't want to wait until it's on his terms."

"It's not that easy—"

McKenzie drew back. "I'm sorry. I shouldn't have asked. You have your brother's wedding and you're leaving town—"

"Do you really think I can leave you now?" He thought of that strange feeling the moment he'd looked into her eyes three nights ago—not to mention the kiss just moments before. He took her hands in his, reveling at the touch of her skin against his. This woman made him feel things he'd never felt before, never dreamed he would ever feel.

"I can't let you go after this man alone. I'm staying until I know you're safe." He wasn't sure he could leave even then and that scared him more than he wanted to admit.

He thought of his brother Tag coming to Montana for Christmas and falling for Lily. Now Tag was getting married and talking about settling in Big Sky. Hayes had thought his brother was nuts to leave behind everything like that.

Hayes felt as if his head were spinning. All he knew for sure was that he had to protect this woman—whatever it took. He couldn't think beyond that, didn't dare.

"I won't be safe as long as he's out there. You said so yourself. I don't see that I have a choice."

A car turned onto the street. The headlights washed over them. Hayes glanced in his rearview mirror as the cop car pulled up behind them.

Hayes didn't have a choice, either. He leaned over and kissed her quickly before climbing out with the note that had been left on her windshield. Like her, he doubted there would be fingerprints on it. Just as he doubted the police would be able to find this man, given how little they had to go on.

The only thing Hayes didn't doubt was that the psycho would be coming for McKenzie.

THE POLICE OFFICER bagged the note her attacker had left and promised to let her know if they found any prints. McKenzie could see that Hayes wasn't holding out any more hope than she was.

The cop walked around the neighborhood, shone his flashlight into the bushes and trees, but to no one's surprise, found nothing.

"He's right," Hayes said after the officer left and he walked her back to her car. "The best thing you can do right now would be to take a long vacation somewhere far away from here."

They stood under Montana's big sky. Millions of stars glittered over their heads and a cool, white moon now buoyed along among them. The June night had turned crisp and cool. This far north even summer nights could chill you. Especially if there was a killer on the loose.

"Do you really think the man would forget about me?" She didn't give him a chance to answer because they both knew that answer. "I can't run away. I would always be looking over my shoulder. No, I have to end this here and soon."

Hayes groaned. "How did I know you were going to say that?"

She shrugged and met his gaze, losing herself in his dark eyes. It would have been easy to get on a plane with him and go to Texas and pretend none of this had happened.

But it *had* happened. Not to mention, she had a business here, people who were counting on her. She wasn't going anywhere—not that Hayes had given her the Texas option to begin with.

She felt strangely calmer as she leaned against the side of her car and looked at the Texas cowboy standing by her. Once she'd settled down enough so she could actually think clearly, she'd made the decision quickly—just as she'd done with her business.

She couldn't wait around for this horrible man to try

to abduct her again and do nothing. If Hayes wouldn't help her, then she would figure out something on her own. She'd been on her own and done all right. She wasn't going to let one crazy psycho change that.

"I have another open house tomorrow." She held up her hand before Hayes could argue. "As you said, he knows who I am. He also knows where I am going to be. For all I know he was one of the people who came through the house earlier. I could have talked to him." She shuddered at the thought and hugged herself.

"I wouldn't be at all surprised that he was one of the men who came through today," Hayes said. "Seeing you feeds whatever it is that drives him. He likes seeing you scared. He'll play with you until he's ready to make his move, until an opportunity presents itself."

She was no fool. She was still scared, but knowing that the man wanted her scared made her determined not to let her fear hold her back. "So you're saying it could be a while before he makes his move?"

"Possibly. Unless you give him the opportunity he needs—like at an open house. You do realize this is speculation based on what I know about men like this. As I said earlier, they're unpredictable. I could be completely off base. There is no way to know what he will do next."

She nodded, considering this. "He feels safe because I didn't see his face the night he attacked me. If you're right about what drives him, he won't be able to stay away."

Hayes took off his Stetson and raked a hand through his thick, dark hair. She recalled the feel of those fingers when he'd taken the nape of her neck in his hand during their kiss.

"If you're determined to do this, then I'm staying down here in the valley tonight. I'm also going to the open house tomorrow," Hayes said.

She shook her head. "He won't make his move as long as you're around."

He stuffed his hat back down on his head and stepped to her to take her shoulders in his hands. "He's just waiting for the chance to get you alone again. He will make that happen with or without me around because he knows I can't watch you all the time. I'll be there tomorrow, like it or not."

McKenzie knew she didn't have the strength to tackle this tonight. "All right," she agreed. She had mixed feelings about having Hayes around. On one hand she would definitely feel safer, but he was a distraction she couldn't afford right now. She had to think clearly.

"He'll come to the open house tomorrow."

Hayes nodded in agreement. "That would be my guess. He's trying to build up his confidence. Being around you and you not knowing how close he is…well, that will make him feel more in control."

"Is there any way to get photos of everyone who comes through the open house?"

"Consider it done. I'll also talk to the police about running the license plates of those who show up."

She smiled at him. "I do appreciate what you're trying to do to keep me safe." She sobered as she looked into his handsome face. "I don't like involving you in this. If this man is as dangerous as we both suspect—"

"Don't worry about me. I'll follow you to your condo. But first let me check your car."

McKenzie watched him look under and around her car before popping the hood and checking the engine. "You can't think he'd put a bomb under my hood."

"Not really. But I do think he might disable your car so it stalls on the way to your condo and while you're trying to figure out what is wrong..."

She got the idea. Distraction. That's how she'd fallen into the man's snare the first time. A memory of the dark night at the grocery-store parking lot flashed before her. She'd been fiddling with her keys, her mind on the phone call and Gus. Gus, she thought with a silent curse. Maybe she should have called the police after she found him on her doorstep at the condo. Was this note merely him trying to scare her? Or was it from the man who'd tried to abduct her?

As she looked out into the darkness, McKenzie wasn't sure who would be caught in the trap she hoped to set for her would-be abductor. Whoever he was, she didn't feel him out there watching her. But he had been there. A psycho who, for whatever reason, had set his sights on her.

AT HER CONDO, McKenzie unlocked the door while Hayes surveyed the neighborhood. He hated that there were too many places for a man to hide. Also, because Bozeman was so small, he had to assume that the man knew where she lived.

He had McKenzie remain by the door until he could check to make sure they were alone in the condo. The place was neat and clean and sparsely furnished. He got the feeling that she didn't spend much time here other than to sleep.

The lower floor consisted of a kitchen, dining room, living room and half bath. Upstairs he found a full bath and two bedrooms. Just the right size for a single woman who worked all the time.

"Can you tell if anyone has been here?" he asked her when he returned to where he'd left her downstairs just inside the door.

She glanced around, clearly startled by the question. "I don't think so. How would he have gotten in?"

"I didn't see any forced entry, but if the man is someone you know and has access to your keys…"

"You mean like an old boyfriend?" She shook her head. "No one has a key to my condo. Nor can I recall anyone having access to my keys."

"Good." He met her gaze. "Do you own a weapon?"

She swallowed and looked uncomfortable. "I have pepper spray, Hayes." His name seemed to come of its own volition. She appeared surprised as if she, too, had just realized that she'd never said it before. "I also have a spare bedroom, if you want to…" She looked away.

"Thanks," he said without hesitation. He was planning to stay, whether she liked it or not.

"The spare bedroom—"

"I know where it is," he said.

She nodded. "I can't take being afraid all the time."

"We'll find him." Even as he said it, Hayes hoped he wasn't promising something he couldn't deliver. He *would* find him, but before the man got to McKenzie? That was what worried him.

She glanced at her watch. "Would you like a drink? I could use one." She headed for the kitchen.

He followed. As she pulled out a bottle of wine from the refrigerator, he said, "I'm going to need to know about everyone who came through the open house today—at least all of them you can remember. Do you have something I can write on?"

She poured them each a glass of wine before removing a notebook and pen from the small desk in the corner of the kitchen. They sat down in the living room on furniture that felt and smelled new. He doubted she had many—if any—guests over, including men. No time to date, he suspected.

That also explained why the man who had attacked her had chosen her. A businesswoman with a lot on her mind. She was a classic case of the perfect female victim. Had the man been following her? Or had he picked her at random? Hayes wished he knew. It would help find the bastard.

"Okay, from when the first person came in after you got to the open house..."

She nodded, took a sip of her wine and began to go through them. He quickly weeded out the women and most of the couples.

"There was that one man near the end..." She stared thoughtfully into space for a moment. "You might have seen him. I was talking to him when you arrived."

Hayes recalled a tall man with a head of thick, brown hair and light-colored eyes. He looked like a former football player. In fact, Hayes recalled wondering if the man had played for the Bobcats while attending Montana State University. He'd been wearing a Bobcat jacket.

"Early forties, big, not bad-looking?"

She nodded. "He seemed interested in the house—until I saw him later when he was leaving."

Hayes frowned. "What changed your mind?"

"You're going to think I'm silly, but he hadn't driven to the open house. I realized he must live in the neighborhood."

"He could have parked some distance away."

She nodded. "I suppose, but as I was watching him walk away, he seemed to sense me watching him and turned. It was his expression… This is where you're going to think I'm nuts, but he turned to look back, right at me as if he knew I would be there watching him, and the look on his face…" She took a drink of her wine. "It was as if he'd put something over on me."

Hayes felt a fissure of unease move through him. "You think it could have been the man who attacked you?"

"He was big enough." She shook her head. "I don't know. He mentioned that he had a wife."

"Probably to put you at ease."

"Maybe. It's just that he seemed…nice, gentle even, almost shy."

"Ted Bundy seemed the same way to *his* victims."

MCKENZIE FINISHED HER wine and poured them both another glass. "Why would he take a chance like that, not just coming to the open house, but actually talking to me?"

"Maybe he wanted to see if you recognized him."

She cupped the wineglass in her hand as she felt a shudder move through her. "Is it possible I was that close to him again and I didn't know it?" That alone terrified her. Could she really not sense the danger?

"It's why the cops take video of people at crime scenes and funerals. Criminals like to return to the scene of the crime. In your case, be close to one of their victims."

"He is safe—until he tries to abduct me again." She shivered. "If he doesn't try again, he'll have gotten away with it." She felt her eyes suddenly widened in alarm. "There have been others, haven't there?"

"More than likely. But that can help. If we find out who this man is, maybe we can place him wherever those other abductions took place."

"You think he *killed* them."

Hayes didn't answer. He didn't have to. "I'm sure the police are looking into other abductions or missing persons around the area.... I'll check with them tomorrow. Tell me about tomorrow's open house."

"It's out in the country. It's fairly...isolated."

"Then I'm definitely going to be there. Don't worry, I'll be discreet. You won't even know I'm around. I'll want to go out earlier than you. Will you be going to your office in the morning even though it's a Sunday?"

"Yes. My job isn't eight to five. Nor five days a week."

"Neither is mine, so I get it," he said, and finished

his wine. His gaze met hers and she felt that bubble of excitement rise inside her, along with a longing that she knew only this man could fill. She wanted him, but not like this. Maybe once this was over…

As if sensing her thoughts, he said, "It's late. We should get some rest." He got to his feet.

"The bed is made up in the spare room. There are towels in the bathroom cabinet…."

"Thank you. I'm sure I have everything I need."

Wasn't that what the man at the open house had said?

Hayes met her gaze. "I'll be right down the hall if you need me."

She nodded. She *did* need him. It was that need that kept her silent as she watched him head upstairs. She heard him go into the bathroom and turn on the shower. She could hear water running and closed her eyes at the thought of Hayes naked in her shower. The Texas cowboy had done something no other man had. He'd reminded her she was a woman, a woman with needs other than her career.

McKenzie poured herself another glass of wine, finishing off the bottle. Normally, she had only one glass before bedtime. Tonight, she didn't mind indulging. Better to indulge in wine than in what she would have liked to indulge in. Her life was complicated enough without getting any more involved with Hayes Cardwell than she already was.

The wine made her feel lightheaded. Or was that her fantasies? Upstairs, Hayes came out of the bathroom. She heard him walk down the hall to the spare bedroom. She waited for him to close the door, but he didn't.

Shutting her eyes, she tried not to think about him lying in bed just down the hall from her own bedroom. A wild yearning raced through her as out of control as a wildfire. Her need quickly became a burning desire as it mixed with the wine already coursing through her veins.

McKenzie had always prided herself on thinking logically. She assessed every situation, looked at it from every angle then made a decision based on the facts—not emotion.

With Hayes, she knew she wasn't thinking rationally. She wanted him, needed him, like no man she'd ever met.

But she wouldn't act on it. Couldn't. At least until the crazy after her was caught. Even then, she wasn't sure she could let herself go. She'd been so wrapped up in her business that she hadn't given much thought to men. Now she couldn't stop thinking about Hayes Cardwell, but she would force herself to. She needed her wits about her and if she gave in to whatever this was between them… The thought made her ache.

She wouldn't let herself go there.

Feeling on moral high ground, she took the empty bottle and the glasses into the kitchen. She tossed the bottle in the trash and hand-washed the glasses, dried them and put them away before she went up to bed. Alone.

HAYES WOKE TO the sound of a phone ringing. He'd had a devil of a time getting to sleep, knowing McKenzie was just down the hall—and that there was a psychopath out there after her. If the man who'd come to the open house was her attacker, then he was definitely brazen. He was practically daring them to catch him.

The phone rang again. He heard McKenzie fumbling to answer it.

"Hello?"

Silence.

"Hello, who is this?"

Hayes was out of bed and down the hall to her room in a matter of a few strides. He reached for the phone. She handed it to him, those amazing eyes of hers wide and terrified. All the color had drained from her face and the hand that relinquished the phone had trembled.

He could hear heavy breathing as he put the phone to his ear. The man on the other end of the line chuckled softly. To his surprise, McKenzie jumped out of bed and ran to the window.

"Who is this?" Hayes demanded.

The chuckle died off. He could almost hear the anger in the breathing just before the call was disconnected. He checked caller ID. Blocked.

"It was him," McKenzie said, turning from the window. She wore a short cotton nightgown that left little to the imagination—not that Hayes's imagination needed any help.

He'd always thought of himself as a strong man. But right now he felt helpless against emotions that threatened to overpower him when he looked at this woman. "McKenzie." He said her name as if that alone could put distance between them and keep him from taking her in his arms.

She turned to him, her voice breaking as she said, “I heard something else besides his breathing.” Her gaze locked with his. “I heard my neighbor’s wind chimes. He called from those pines below my bedroom window.”

Chapter Nine

Gus Thompson was lost. He'd driven around town tonight feeling as if his life were over. The last place he'd wanted to go was home to an empty house. He still couldn't believe everything had changed in an instant.

He was thirty-eight years old. Not even in his prime. He would get another job. At least that's what he told himself. And yet just the thought of approaching other Realtors had turned his knees to jelly. He'd never had to actually ask for a job before. His mother had seen that he had jobs from the time he was sixteen. Nepotism wasn't something he'd ever thought about—until now.

If his mother were alive, she would have put in a call, got him on somewhere and he'd just show up for work. She'd had those kinds of connections. Even better, his mother would have made McKenzie pay. Her wrath would have rained down like a firestorm on M.K. Realty. She might even have put dear McKenzie out of business just for spite.

But his mother was gone and he was jobless and lost. And all because of McKenzie Sheldon.

He hadn't known where he was driving until he

found himself in her neighborhood. Parking down the block, he'd cut the engine, having no idea what he was going to do when she returned. Their "talk" earlier had left him cold. He needed more from her than a lukewarm recommendation. He was a great salesman, but if there were even a whiff of gossip that he was difficult to work with or that he hit on women in the office, it would kill the deal.

McKenzie had to hire him back. It was the only way.

As that thought settled over him, he'd seen her come up the street and pull into her drive. He'd started to get out, afraid how far he would have to go to get her to agree to rehire him, when an SUV had pulled up in her drive next to her vehicle.

Gus had ducked back into his car as he watched the Texas cowboy get out. McKenzie and the man headed for her front door. "What the—" They'd disappeared inside. A few minutes later, the cowboy had come back out and driven his vehicle into her garage.

It was the same cowboy he'd seen her with at Big Sky. The same man he'd followed to the Cardwell Ranch only to have neither appear again even after Gus had waited an hour.

Determined to wait this time, though, he settled in. The cowboy would leave before daylight, he told himself. He must have fallen asleep because something awakened him. He sat up to find it was the middle of the night. All the lights were off inside the condo—just like the other condos on the block.

Angry and frustrated and feeling even worse, he was about to leave when he noticed something odd. A man had been sitting in an old panel van up the street. Gus watched him get out and head into the trees next to McKenzie's condo. A few moments later, Gus saw a light flash in the trees. Not like a flashlight. More like a small screen, making Gus suspect the man was making a call on his cell phone next to her condo.

How many men did McKenzie have on the string? he wondered. Definitely the cowboy.

So who was the man in the trees? His heart began to pound as he realized it could be the same guy who'd attacked her.

Before he could react, the man came out of the trees, walking fast. He jumped into the van. Gus hurriedly started his car, a plan crystallizing as he drove. If this guy was McKenzie's attacker and he could catch him, she would have to give him back his job.

HAYES, DRESSED ONLY in jeans, ran back to his room and grabbed his gun after the call and what McKenzie had heard on the other end of the line. He raced down the stairs and out the front door. If she was right, the man had been right outside her condo in the dense trees.

But as he reached the trees, he heard tires squeal and looked out on the street as a large car sped past. This time, though, the car passed under a streetlamp and he was able to get the license plate number.

Back in the condo, he found McKenzie wrapped in a fluffy white robe and matching slippers. She stood hugging herself at the front window.

"Did you…" Her words died off as she saw his expression. "He got away."

"I got his license plate number as he was speeding off." Hayes was already dialing the police. He asked for the same officer who they'd talked to earlier and told him about the phone call and the car.

"Give me a minute," the cop said as he ran the plate. "The car belongs to Ruth Thompson. Wait a minute. It's the same car Gus Thompson admitted to driving the night Ms. Sheldon was attacked."

"She has a restraining order on him."

"I see that. I'll make sure he gets picked up."

"Thank you." Hayes hung up and turned to look at McKenzie. "Did you actually see him in the trees?"

She shook her head. "He was just a shape. Large."

"The car that I saw racing away was Gus Thompson's mother's." She groaned. "Is it possible he also made the phone call?"

She seemed to think for a moment. "The man didn't say anything, he just…breathed." She closed her eyes and sighed. "It would be like Gus to try to torment me. He's furious that I fired him. So you think it wasn't the man who attacked me?"

"Not unless that man was Gus Thompson."

"WHAT THE DEVIL?" He looked in his rearview mirror, surprised that the car he'd seen earlier was still following him. He knew it couldn't be either McKenzie Sheldon or the cowboy he'd seen her with before. So who was it?

Not the police or they would have already pulled him over.

He had spotted the tail right away, but hadn't thought

anything of it. He had too much on his mind to care. What was the cowboy doing at her house? He could only imagine. He gritted his teeth, remembering the male voice on the phone. The Texas accent had been a dead giveaway. It had to be the same cowboy, the one who'd rescued her at the grocery-store parking lot. The same one he'd seen her with before. And now the man was in her condo with her? Close enough he'd gotten on her *phone?*

A wave of disgust and fury washed over him like acid on his skin. He'd never taken women out of any kind of anger. If anything, it was about control. So this scalding fury made him feel impotent. He had to do something about this situation and soon.

But how could he get control again—and quickly? If he acted out in anger, he would be more likely to make a mistake, one that could cost him dearly. No, he had to rein in his emotions. He couldn't let this woman and her hero cowboy get to him.

But even as he'd thought it, he felt his blood boiling. How dare the two of them! It was as if they were laughing behind his back. Mocking him. Now the cowboy had something that belonged to him. The woman was *his,* not some stupid bystander's who'd come to her rescue.

He had to think, plan. The woman had known he was outside her window. How? He remembered the way she'd stood at the window at the open house, watching him leave. He'd sensed her watching him. Had she also sensed how close he was to her tonight?

Or had it been something else? That's when he

remembered the wind chimes. He'd noticed them when he'd been waiting in the trees. They had been tinkling lightly so he hadn't paid much attention. But right when she'd answered the phone, a gust had caught them… *She'd heard the wind chimes.* The woman was more astute than any of the others, a worthier prey. It should have filled him with pride since she was now his.

The only thing spoiling it was the cowboy.

He thought of how he'd planned it, borrowing the old van he sometimes used at work, waiting until she'd be asleep before he'd called. He'd wanted to wake her, to catch her off guard. He hadn't known she wouldn't be alone.

A curse on his lips, he glanced again in his rearview mirror. The car was still with him! The driver had been staying back, but clearly following him. It was one reason he hadn't gone home. Instead, he'd been driving around, trying to clear his head and ditch the tail. But the fool was still with him.

It couldn't be the cowboy, could it? No. Then who? He reached under the seat for the tire iron he kept there, and was about to throw on his brakes and see just who was following him when he caught the flash of cop lights behind them.

Fear turned his blood to slush—until he realized that the cop wasn't after him, but whoever had been following him. He kept driving up another block before he turned and circled back. He had to know who'd seen him at the condo. Who was stupid enough to put himself in jeopardy?

Fortunately, as he drove by, neither the cop nor the

man bent over his car's hood being handcuffed paid any attention to him.

The man being arrested wasn't the Texas cowboy, but he did look familiar.

AFTER HAYES LEFT the condo this morning, McKenzie locked the door behind him as he'd ordered. She was still upset that the man who'd called last night had been right outside her condo. *He knew where she lived!*

But if the man was Gus… She still couldn't believe that even though the police had called to tell her that the car Hayes had seen speeding away belonged to Gus Thompson and that Gus had been arrested, but was expected to be out on bail soon.

"I really don't like you doing this open house," Hayes had said this morning before he left. "This nutcase is going to strike when you least expect it."

"Then I will have to be on guard all the time."

Once ready for the open house, she called to remind him that she had to stop at her office.

"I'll meet you there," he said.

"That really isn't necessary."

"I'll be the judge of that."

Only Cynthia and another real-estate saleswoman were in the office this morning. The others either had open houses or had taken the day off. She'd always felt a sense of euphoria when she walked into her office. She'd worked hard for this agency and felt a sense of pride that she'd done it alone through hard work.

But today she felt edgy. She couldn't forget for a moment that she was being hunted like an animal. It set her nerves on end and made her start whenever the phone rang.

McKenzie knew she had to pull it together. Last night she'd been angry, filled with a determination to track down this bastard and stop him. But in the light of day, she was too aware of how ill-prepared she was. She'd gotten lucky the other night and had been able to fight the man off—at least long enough that Hayes had seen what was going on and had saved her.

She couldn't count on his saving her again. That's what he was trying to tell her earlier at the condo.

And yet when she saw him drive up, she'd never been so happy to see anyone. "I told you I was driving myself," she said, glancing at the clock. The open house wouldn't start for several hours.

"There's somewhere we need to go." He sounded mysterious, but she followed him out to his SUV and climbed in. He drove out into the country, down a narrow dirt road until they were back into the foothills away from town.

When he stopped, she glanced around. "What are we doing?"

"You really think you're ready for this?" he asked as he pulled out a gun.

She felt her eyes widen in alarm. He held the gun out to her. "You ever fired one before? I didn't think so. You think you can kill someone?"

"Is this really necessary? I have pepper spray that I carry—"

"Pepper spray isn't going to stop this guy. I've seen the way you grip your keys when you get out of the car.

If he gets close enough to grab you, your keys aren't going to stop him, either. You're going to have to kill him or he is going to kill you."

She stared at the gun for a moment. Then she swallowed the lump in her throat as she reached for it. Her hand trembled. She stilled it as she got a good grip on the pistol.

"Will you show me how to fire it?"

He'd raised a brow. "You really think you can do this?"

"I don't think I have a choice, do you?"

He took the gun from her. "Come on, then." Climbing out he led the way to a gully where he set up a half-dozen rusted beer cans on rocks. "Familiarize yourself with the gun. Here is how you load it. Here is how you fire it."

Turning toward the cans, he showed her how to hold the gun and take aim. She did as he had done, looked down the barrel and pulled the trigger. The gun kicked in her hand, the shot going wild.

"Don't close your eyes when you pull the trigger," he said.

She tried again, holding the gun tighter. The next shot was closer. The third one pinged into a can, knocking it to the ground. She felt a surge of satisfaction, missed the next shot, but centered the cans on the next two.

Feeling cocky, she turned to look at him. "Well?"

"You killed a few old beer cans. You will have only a split second to make the decision whether to pull the trigger or not—and that's if you can pull the gun fast enough when the man surprises you," Hayes said. "He'll be counting on those few seconds when you hesitate."

"WHERE ARE YOU?" Tag asked, not long before noon. "I checked your cabin. It hasn't been slept in."

Hayes was driving north, leaving Bozeman and traveling out into the country past wheat fields broken by subdivisions. "I stayed at McKenzie's last night. Quit smirking. Nothing happened—at least not what you're thinking."

"Oh?"

He found the road he needed and turned down it. The sun had cleared the mountains to the east this morning and now splashed the valley in gold. "This guy who attacked her is still after her. She's determined to find him before he finds her. I'm helping her."

"Did you read something on a fortune cookie that says if you save someone's life, you're responsible for it?"

"I can't just leave her," Hayes said as he saw the house come into view.

"Really? That's all it is, just you needing to play hero?"

"I can't get into this right now. I'll call you as soon as I know something definite, but I might be staying until your wedding. Also, I told McKenzie we will take the restaurant building at Big Sky. I haven't talked to Austin but—"

"Was this McKenzie Sheldon's doing? Never mind. Whatever the reason you've changed your mind, I'm glad. You won't be sorry."

"I hope not."

"Now try not to get yourself killed before my wedding."

As Tag hung up, Hayes sped up the SUV, driving past the house and up the road for a half mile before he turned around and headed back, going slower this time.

The ranch-style house was huge, sprawled across twenty acres with a guesthouse, barn and stables behind it, along with an assortment of outbuildings. All kinds of places for a person to hide. He noticed there was also a dirt road that went up into the Bridger Mountains behind the house.

As he drove on by the house a second time, he called McKenzie. "Get someone to do the open house for you. It's too dangerous."

Gus had been arrested last night for violating the restraining order. But McKenzie had received a call earlier, warning her that he was already out on bail.

What had Hayes upset was what else the policewoman had told her. "He swears he saw a man beside your condo last night using a cell phone. He says he was chasing the man when he was arrested."

"Did he get a good look at the man?" McKenzie had asked.

"He says he didn't."

The policewoman hadn't believed Gus about any of it.

Hayes didn't know what to believe. Gus could be behind both the note on McKenzie's car and the call last night. Gus was angry, according to the police, which gave him reason to want to torment his former boss, even if he wasn't the man who'd attacked her.

"It wasn't Gus," she'd again said this morning on the drive back from shooting the gun.

"But Gus would know about the convention speech and the open house," Hayes had argued. "And he was definitely at your condo last night."

"You said he sped away. You didn't see another car?"

He hadn't been looking for another car once he'd seen Gus speeding away.

"I went by Gus Thompson's house," he said now. "He's not there. This open house is in the paper with your name on it, right?"

"It's not Gus."

"Okay, then if true, I would say you have two angry men after you now. Which is yet another reason you shouldn't do the open house."

"The police are going to have a car in the area of the open house."

"The area is too large and there are too many places a man could be hiding."

"*You'll* be there."

Her words hit him at heart level. "Why do you think I'm so worried?"

"I trust you."

Her first mistake. He opened his mouth to speak, but shook his head, instead. A part of him was touched by her words. Another part was afraid he would fail her.

"Hayes?"

"I'm still here."

"I know. I'm grateful."

He sighed. "Let me know when you leave the office for the open house. Keep your phone on. I won't stop worrying until I know you made the drive safely. Then, once you get here, I can really start worrying."

"So you agree with me that he'll show?"

"He'll be here. He couldn't possibly pass up such a perfect location with all these places to hide. The question is where."

GUS WAS NO longer angry at McKenzie. He was *furious.* She hadn't really had him *arrested?* Not when he was following the man who he assumed had attacked her.

When he'd first gotten released from jail he'd thought about just letting the crazy bastard get her. She deserved it, right?

After a while, though, he'd tamped down his fury, focusing instead on the look he'd see on her face when he caught her stalker. When he *saved* her.

He dug the handgun from the drawer beside his bed. He'd bought the pistol at a gun show years ago. The gun was loaded, but he grabbed another box of ammunition.

As he walked through the kitchen, he grabbed a sharp knife. He put the knife in the top of his boot. Today he'd worn jeans, hiking boots, a long-sleeved shirt. He had some dirty business to get done today.

In the garage, he walked past his mother's car to his SUV. He felt like a commando going into battle. The man after McKenzie had been at her condo last night. That had been a gutsy move. So Gus figured, given where the open house was being held, that the man would show. All Gus had to do was get there early for a place to hide out and wait. It would be like shooting fish in a bucket—barrel, whatever.

He'd checked out the house and grounds when the ranchette had first come on the market, so he knew where to park the SUV so it wouldn't be noticed. There was literally a forest that backed up to the property. He knew the perfect spot where he would be able to see anyone coming.

McKENZIE GREW MORE anxious as she neared the ranchette. She remembered what Hayes had said last night. But her car seemed to be running fine. However, she was relieved when she reached the turnoff to the house.

She didn't see Hayes anywhere around, but then again, she didn't expect to. He was here, though, she assured herself. The property was twenty acres, just as Hayes had said. While she'd seen the place before, she found herself looking at it from a totally different perspective than she had the first time.

Now she saw all the places a man could hide and wait for that moment when she was alone. And she would be alone some of the time because the asking price of this place was high enough that she didn't expect a lot of viewers.

Fear rippled over her, dimpling her skin and giving her a chill as she got out at the turnoff to put up the Open House sign. She couldn't help looking over her shoulder, hurrying to get the sign up and back into her vehicle as quickly as possible.

She was shaking by the time she climbed behind the wheel again. Did she really think she could do this? To catch this man she would eventually have to come face-to-face with him. He had to be caught in action. Her heart began to pound at the memory of his arm around her throat, the way he'd picked her up off her feet—

Turning down the road, she heard another vehicle. An SUV turned down the long drive behind her. She glanced at the car's clock. Her first viewer was early. As she pulled in, she saw that the car had slowed as if to study the place at a distance. Hurrying, she climbed out, taking everything with her as she moved toward the empty house. Her heart hammered in her chest as she opened the door and felt a blast of stale, cold air hit her.

She had to calm down. Taking a few breaths, she reminded herself how far she'd come. She hadn't gotten her success by being a wimp. She straightened her back as she put down the flyers and turned to watch the SUV cruise slowly up the road toward her. The sun glinted off the windshield so she couldn't see the driver.

This could be him.

Or he could already be in the house waiting for me.

Chapter Ten

Last night had been a close call. Some fool had chased him. Fortunately, the police had pulled the man over. He'd gotten a good look at the man's familiar face but it wasn't until he got home that he placed him. He'd seen Gus Thompson's face enough times when he'd been perusing the real-estate ads looking for McKenzie Sheldon's smiling face.

Just the thought of her made him feel better. But he couldn't ignore the fact that the man had given him chase last night. Did McKenzie now have *two* men protecting her? That made his stomach roil. It was bad enough that the cowboy kept getting in his way. Now this other fool?

To settle himself down, he thought about the open house and Ms. Sheldon. He would see her again today. Unfortunately, just seeing her wasn't helping much anymore. He needed more. He smiled in memory of the terror he'd seen on McKenzie Sheldon's face last night when she'd found the note and what he'd heard in her voice when he'd called and woken her up.

But even that wasn't enough. He had to get his hands on her.

True, she had needed a reminder that he was still here, that he was still coming for her. It had been a dangerous thing to do, calling attention to himself that way. But he relished in the fear, both his own and, of course, hers.

He'd been curious to see, after the note and the phone call, whether or not she would go ahead with the open house today. The listing was out in the country, miles from town and enough acreage and buildings that not even her cowboy or Gus Thompson, real-estate salesman extraordinaire, could keep her safe.

She'd proven to be a worthy opponent. But today would tell if the woman was equal to the challenge.

He'd already decided that he had to show up at the open house. She might be suspicious of him after yesterday since he'd been one of only a handful of men who'd come alone to the open house.

Today he would assure her she had nothing to fear from him.

After all, the one thing he could do well was *act* normal. He'd spent his life fooling people—even those closest to him. He knew exactly how he would play it and couldn't wait.

HAYES FELT HIS stomach tighten as viewers began to arrive. When he'd spoken to the police earlier, they'd agreed to run the plates of those attending the open house. They'd asked the sheriff's department to send a car out to the area, as well.

Given the price of this so-called ranchette, he'd thought that number would be low. He'd been surprised by the turnout.

Most were just curious, he was betting. But some actually appeared to be interested, walking much of the grounds, looking in the many structures. He'd heard that expensive houses in the area had continued to sell, even during the recession. It was easy to understand why people fell in love with Bozeman's charm, along with the beautiful valley, the nearby mountains and inexhaustible outdoor entertainment.

He took down each license plate number and snapped a photo of the people attending. He had a half dozen written down when the man drove up. He recognized the man right away as the one he'd seen talking to McKenzie the day before at the open house. Was this her attacker? He was dressed in jeans, boots and a Western shirt and had a cocky way about him.

As the man climbed out of his SUV, he glanced around as if taking in the place for the first time, then he headed for the front door.

MCKENZIE HAD BEEN talking to a middle-aged couple and turned to find the man directly behind her.

"I'm sorry. I didn't mean to startle you." He held out his hand. "Bob Garwood."

McKenzie battled back her initial surprise and took his hand. It was cool to the touch, the handshake firm. She even found her voice. "It's nice to meet you, Mr. Garwood."

"Please, call me Bob." He let go of her hand and

glanced around the living area. "I like this much better than yesterday's listing. How many acres?"

"Twenty. Most of it is now leased for hay."

He nodded. "That's great." His gaze came back to hers. "Mind if I take one of those?"

She handed him a sales flyer. Her hand was hardly shaking.

"Sheldon, right? McKenzie Sheldon. I almost called you last night. You gave me your card with your cell phone number, remember?"

She nodded numbly. If this was the man who'd attacked her, then he *had* called her last night. In fact, he'd been outside her condo. Her heart began to pound harder.

He smiled. "This might seem a little forward, but I wanted to ask you to dinner sometime."

"I don't date clients."

His smile broadened as he pulled out his card and handed it to her. "Good thing I'm not a client yet."

With that he walked away, his gaze going from the sales flyer in his hand to the house as if he seriously was looking for something to buy. She glanced down at the card. Robert Garwood. Apparently, he sold high-tech workout equipment for gyms.

"Are you all right?"

She jumped before she recognized the voice and turned to find Hayes behind her. "How long have you been here?"

"Long enough to hear him ask you for a date."

She let out a nervous laugh. "Maybe that's all he was doing, just hitting on me."

"Maybe. I'll run his name. Bob Garwood, right?"

She nodded as a few more cars pulled up out front. Two women climbed out of one vehicle, a couple out of another and one man, alone.

"You remember him from yesterday's open house?" Hayes asked.

The men's faces were all starting to blend together. "I think so."

"I'll be close by if you need me," he whispered and left.

McKenzie braced herself as the man who'd just arrived looked up at the house, then started up the walk. She recognized him as being one from yesterday's open house. As she took a closer look at the couple, she realized the husband also looked familiar.

"Holler if you need me," Hayes said and left out the back way.

McKenzie jumped as the front door opened. She plastered a smile on her face as the group entered. The lone man took a flyer, gave her a nod and moved off through the house behind the two women. The husband she recognized from the day before came up to her.

"You're a busy woman," he said. "Didn't I see you yesterday at an open house in town?"

She nodded, wondering if he really didn't remember. He was large and there was something about his light blue eyes that made her feel naked. He was the one who'd acted as if he was pulling something on her yesterday.

His gaze locked with hers and she felt a shiver move

through her. She tried to repress it as she handed him a sales flyer.

He nodded, his gaze still on her as if he was trying to place her.

McKenzie tried to pull herself together. She'd been so determined last night, so sure she wanted to trap the man. But being this close to a possible suspect…

He was still looking at her.

"Jason?"

"Sorry," he said, turning to the woman with him. "I was just lost in thought for a minute there." He let out a self-deprecating laugh. "I'm Jason Mathews. This is my wife, Emily."

She shook the wife's hand, then Jason Mathews's. He had a firm handshake and held her hand a little too long, making her even more nervous.

"I was surprised when Jason suggested we buy something larger," Emily said. She was a small woman with dark hair and eyes. Her handshake had been limp and cold. As she spoke, she kept looking at her husband. "We own a house in town that's paid for, but I would love a place in the country. This might be too much for us, though. I hate to even ask what it costs."

Jason Mathews smiled at his wife. "Well, let's have a look. You might be surprised what we can afford." He gave McKenzie a conspiratorial wink and handed her his card before leading his wife toward the kitchen.

McKenzie tried to catch her breath as she glanced down at the card in her hand. Jason Mathews. Under his name was: Antiquities Appraiser and his business number.

She groaned inwardly as she realized how foolish she had been. The man apparently really was interested in buying a house. With a sigh, she turned to welcome more people into the house.

But every man who came in alone to see the ranchette made her wonder if he was the one she had to fear.

THERE WERE TOO many people here. He finally found himself alone next to one of the outbuildings and took a breath. He couldn't believe how smooth he'd been when he'd seen McKenzie Sheldon again. It had taken some of the sting out of failing. He couldn't wait to get her alone.

Talking to McKenzie Sheldon had his blood running hot, though. He felt his need growing, worse this time because of his failure. Just the thought of his hands on her bare skin— The things he would make her do. The things he would do to her.

A flash of light caught his attention. He stepped back into the shade of the building and cupped his hands to look up the hillside toward the forest. There was someone up there in the barn loft. The flash must have been binoculars. A cop? Or that damned cowboy?

He'd known the cowboy would be here protecting McKenzie. It irritated him, but would give him such satisfaction when he stole the woman from the cowboy right in front of his eyes. He smiled just thinking about it.

In the shadow of the building, he waited and watched, hoping for a glimpse of whoever was hiding up in the barn loft. Finally, his patience paid off. He caught a glimpse of a face and swore.

It was that man who'd followed him last night from McKenzie's condo, the same man he'd witnessed getting arrested. Obviously, Gus Thompson had gotten out of jail.

He didn't need to speculate on who the man was looking for. Stupid fool.

A hot well of need rushed through his blood. The women he took fulfilled a variety of his needs on several levels. At first, killing them had been just a precaution, but over time he'd begun to enjoy that part, as well.

If he couldn't have McKenzie just yet, well, maybe he could satisfy at least one of his yearnings.

GUS CAUGHT MOVEMENT out of the corner of his eye. He had found the perfect spot in the barn loft. Through a small window, he had been able to watch the property as well as the comings and goings at the house. He'd picked the barn because he'd known that few people would come all the way up the hillside to the big barn, let alone climb up to the hayloft.

A few had made the hike but only given the barn a cursory look. The stables were much more interesting, and even some of the outbuildings. But since the place was immaculate, all the buildings painted white with dark green trim, it was easy to see that everything was well maintained.

He could sell this place in a heartbeat, he thought with aching regret. What did McKenzie know about selling this property? It should have been his listing.

He was thinking that when he saw movement off to his right in the pine trees. Gus turned, fear making his movement jerky. He'd forgotten why he was here for a moment and that kind of distraction was just when the man who had attacked McKenzie would take advantage.

But to his surprise, there was no one in the pines next to the barn. The breeze stirred the branches, casting shadows over the dry needles on the ground.

He reminded himself that he couldn't get caught here by anyone or he would be going back to jail.

He might have convinced himself that he'd imagined the movement if he hadn't heard a sound below him. As his heart began to pound, he pulled the pistol he'd brought and moved cautiously toward the hole in the floor where the ladder came up.

He'd lied to the cops about the man he'd seen at McKenzie's condo. Even though it had been dark and the man had been dressed in a hooded black sweatshirt, he'd gotten a pretty decent look at him in the streetlamp. Once he saw him again, he'd know him.

He heard nothing below him. He thought about going down the ladder when he realized there was another way up into the loft—a second ladder on the other side of the large stack of hay.

Gun ready, he cautiously moved in that direction. The smell of the hay and dust filled his nostrils. As the floor beneath his feet creaked, he couldn't hold back the sneeze. He stopped and listened again. No sound other than the breeze in the pines nearby.

There was no one. He felt both relieved and disappointed. His only hope of getting his job back was saving McKenzie, he thought as he heard a slight rustle in the stack of hay next to him.

HAYES MENTALLY KICKED himself as he walked the perimeter of the property one last time. The open house had ended almost an hour ago but there were some visitors who were just now leaving. He'd texted McKenzie just moments ago. She'd texted back that she was fine. He tried to relax since the stragglers were either couples or several groups of women. No lone male. At least not one who he'd seen.

Earlier he'd found tracks coming from the road behind the house. But with the property bordering the forest, there were too many places to hide for him to search for a vehicle. He couldn't be sure that the tracks weren't from the owner or one of the people viewing the house and property.

He'd also found a place where someone had stood for a while on a rise with a view of the house. The boot tracks were men-sized, but they could belong to anyone. He felt as if he were looking for a needle in a haystack. He couldn't even be sure the man who'd attacked McKenzie was even here.

Since arming her with the gun, he'd had his misgivings. The gun had been more about making him feel better than any real protection for her. Now he hoped he hadn't made things worse and she shot some innocent fool who surprised her.

But he couldn't watch her all the time. Was it wrong to want her to have a fighting chance? Whether or not the gun would give her that...well, he couldn't say. It would all depend on when her attacker decided to strike again.

He was about to head for the house when something

caught his eye. For a moment, he almost ignored it. He was anxious to get to McKenzie. The last of the viewers were leaving. That would mean she was alone.

Staring up at the barn, he saw what had drawn his attention. The barn had four small octagonal windows across one side on the loft level. He saw now that there was something in one of the barn windows that hadn't been there earlier.

Hayes glanced down the hillside toward the house, torn. Whatever was in the barn window probably was nothing. He needed to get to McKenzie. And yet… He quickly texted her.

Everyone gone?

Yes.

He could almost feel the relief in that one word.

Lock all the doors and wait for me.

Pocketing his phone, he walked quickly up the hillside toward the barn.

Earlier it had been hot, but now with the waning sun, the air felt cool. He could smell the pines, hear the breeze rustling the boughs. As he neared the barn, he slowed. A prickling at his neck made him pull his weapon before he stepped into the cool, hollow darkness.

The inside of the barn was empty. He glanced overhead to the loft, then at the ladder. There was fresh manure on several of the steps. Someone had been up there, someone who'd come in through the corral where the horses were kept.

At the foot of the ladder, he saw that there was another way up into the loft—a second set of stairs, these much easier to climb. Moving to them, he began to climb, the only sound inside the cavernous barn the pounding of his heart.

Hayes slowed near the top, weapon ready. The moment he peered over the top, he saw the man sprawled on the loft floor, the strewn hay around him discolored with the man's blood.

As he eased up through the opening to the loft floor, he saw that the man's throat had been sliced from ear to ear. From the color of the blood straining the hay, he hadn't been dead long.

Hayes hurriedly surveyed the area, then careful not to contaminate the scene, checked the man's wallet and identification.

Gus Thompson, the man McKenzie had fired.

Chapter Eleven

As Hayes came through the door, McKenzie turned, clearly startled. Hayes saw her hand go to the gun in her bag, but stop short when she recognized him. Relief washed over her features as she dropped the bag and stepped into his arms.

"You're shaking," he said as he hugged her to him.

"The deputies wouldn't tell me anything, just to stay in the house. I saw the ambulance. I was so afraid it was you. What happened?"

"It's Gus Thompson. I found him in the barn on the property."

"Gus?"

"He's dead. He was…murdered."

McKenzie shook her head in obvious disbelief as she stepped out of his embrace. *"Murdered?"*

"The sheriff's department is investigating. That's all I can tell you."

She looked as stunned as he'd been when he'd ID'd the dead man. "What was Gus…?"

"Your guess is as good as mine."

"If he was the one who attacked me…" Her voice trailed off. "He wasn't."

"It doesn't appear so, but he definitely seemed to be stalking you. It could be he crossed paths with your attacker."

"So my attacker was here! He was someone who came through the house."

"Maybe. As I told you, with a property this size, he may have sneaked onto the place without anyone seeing him."

"Except Gus." She shivered. "I can't believe he's dead."

"I'm sure the deputies will want to question you about who came through the open house."

"But I don't know *anything.* A half-dozen men came through alone, but that isn't unusual."

"What about that man who asked you out? Bob Garwood."

She shook her head. "He's not the first man who came to an open house hoping to get a date with the Realtor. There were other men who could have been the one who attacked me." She described several of the men who'd come through. "There was one, Jason Mathews. He gave me a funny feeling, but he came through with his wife, Emily, so…."

"I'll check him out along with the others but there is a good chance the man who killed Gus didn't come into the house."

"You took down all the license plate numbers?"

"I did. I've turned them over to the sheriff's department." He hated to get her hopes up. If he was right about this man, the killer had gone years learning how to not get caught. He was good at this and he knew it. "We might get lucky, though."

McKenzie had stopped trembling, but she was still shocked and shaken. After she'd talked to the deputies, Hayes had followed her back to her condo. She'd worked so hard, determined to be successful and independent. She hadn't wanted to need anyone. Now her carefully built world was coming apart at the seams, and it scared her more than she wanted to admit how dependent she'd become on Hayes Cardwell.

She had to get control of her life again. That meant she needed answers—even those she knew she didn't want to hear. "You said you were going to do some research to see if other women... There have been others, haven't there?"

"Maybe you should sit down," he suggested as they moved into the living room.

She shook her head, crossing her arms over her chest as if she could hold back the fear that filled her. "Just tell me."

"More than two dozen have disappeared over the last ten years. The more recent ones match your profile."

"*My* profile?"

"Successful, single businesswomen who work late, shop late, have a lot on their plates."

She tried to swallow the lump in her throat. "I'm his type, that's what you're saying. Did any of them...?"

"None got away. I believe you might be the first."

"Then they are all..."

"Still missing."

She tried not to imagine the other women. "In other words, they're probably dead." She waited, seeing that he knew more than he was telling her.

"Several have turned up in shallow graves. They all went missing mostly out West. I suspect this man travels with his job. Since you have been the only one who he attempted to abduct in this area, I think there is a good chance that he lives here." At her frown, he added, "Predators don't normally hunt in their backyards. Too dangerous."

"But he *did.*"

Hayes nodded. "With what I know about his type, he probably can go for a length of time and then something just snaps or builds to the point where he can't help himself."

"So I just happened to be in the wrong place at the wrong time."

"Probably."

"But now he knows who I am and if I'm the only one that ever got away…"

"That's why you can't stay here."

She shook her head. "How long do you think I can hide from him, Hayes? I have a business to run. I need to work."

He shook his head. "I don't have all the answers."

"I know." She looked into his kind, handsome face. He hadn't asked for any of this. All she wanted to do was bury her face in his strong chest. In his arms, she felt safe. But Hayes wouldn't always be there to hold her and protect her. It was one reason she had to know everything she could about the man after her.

"You talked to the police about Gus?" She saw the answer on his face. "Tell me."

"The coroner said Gus was hit with a piece of pipe. The blow wasn't enough to kill him, but probably knocked him down, at least stunned him long enough for the killer to..." Hayes met her gaze. "Are you sure you want to hear this?"

"I got the man killed."

"That's not true and you know it. You had a restraining order against him. If Gus had stayed away, he would still be alive today."

She stepped to the window, her back to him, her mind reeling. "What was Gus doing in that barn?"

"The police think he was spying on you. They found binoculars near the window and a bag with candy bars. It was the bag I saw in the window fluttering in the breeze that made me go up to the barn. He had hooked it on a nail next to him. When the breeze came up..."

She turned to look at him. "Why would he spy on me?"

"You said he wanted to talk to you. Maybe he thought he could get you alone and convince you to give him back his job." Hayes shook his head. "Who knows."

"The police think his killer was the man who tried to abduct me, don't they?" She didn't wait for him to confirm it. "Gus swore to the police that he followed him last night after the man called me from down in the pines by the wind chimes. If he was telling the truth, maybe he wasn't there spying on me but looking for the man. But why would Gus do something like that?"

"Maybe he wanted to play hero and it got him killed."

"If he was looking for my attacker, that means he could recognize him. *Gus lied to the police.*" That shouldn't have surprised her. It would be just like Gus. Tears filled her eyes. "This is all because I fired him."

Hayes stepped to her and took her in his arms. She didn't fight it. She rested her cheek against his chest, soaking in his warmth, hoping to chase away the chill that had settled in her, even for a little while.

"McKenzie, none of this is your fault. Gus made some very poor decisions. That's what got him killed."

"Playing hero, isn't that what you called it?" she asked as she pulled back to look into his dark eyes. "So anyone who tries to protect me—"

"Don't," he said, as if seeing where she was headed with this.

She shook her head and stepped away from him. "He'll come after you next. I can't let that happen."

"I'm not Gus. He wasn't trained for this. I am."

"I want you to go back to Texas."

"AIN'T HAPPENIN'," HAYES said. "I'm staying right here and there is nothing you can do to drive me away, so don't even try."

She looked up at him, her eyes brimming with tears. "I couldn't bear it if anything happened to you because of me."

He reached her in two long strides and took her shoulders in his hands. "Nothing is going to happen to me. Or to you. We are going to catch this guy." He could see that she didn't believe that. He wondered if he did himself.

"I thought if we set a trap for him... I thought today..." Tears spilled down her cheeks. She had a swipe at them. "It was a stupid idea and look what happened because of me."

He could see her fighting to be strong. He'd never met a more courageous woman. "It wasn't stupid. He was there, just as you'd thought he would be. Unfortunately, Gus was, too. Listen, I have a plan. It's dangerous—"

She laughed, but there was no humor in it. "More dangerous than waiting around for him to attack me again after what he did today?"

"If I am right about this man, he's had some experience at this. He'll *expect* a trap. He knows the police and now sheriff's department are involved. I'm sure he knows I'm involved, as well."

"What are you saying? That he'll lie low for a while?"

He nodded. He didn't want to tell her that killing Gus would have relieved some of the killer's...tension. The man would be satisfied for a while. "But whatever drives him will eventually reach the point where—"

"He'll try to grab some other woman!"

"No. He can't move on until he's finished with you."

"You don't know that."

"Not positively, but based on what I know about these types of predators..." He held her gaze. "But understand. The longer he goes, the more dangerous he will be."

"Then you need to go back to Texas. Like you said, he knows you're involved. If he killed Gus because he thought he was in the way…"

"Who knows what happened with Gus. The truth is, I believe you're the only one who will be able to satisfy his need."

McKenzie swallowed. "This plan you have…"

"Right now, you're too accessible. He can fill some of his need too easily by simply seeing you and seeing that you're afraid or cutting off part of your hair as a souvenir. You need to hide out for a while. The longer we let him dangle, the more his confidence will decline. He won't know where you've gone. Then when you surface again…he'll make mistakes."

She felt her eyes fill with tears. "At least that's what you're hoping for."

He nodded, not telling her what else he was hoping for.

"So I hide out until…until what?"

"Until he can't take it any longer." Hayes pulled her into his arms and stroked her back. He was hoping that he would find the bastard before that happened. "You have to trust me." He drew back to look into her eyes. "Do you trust me, McKenzie?"

She nodded.

"Then the two of us are going to Cardwell Ranch."

HE LICKED AT a spot of blood on his wrist that he'd missed and smiled. When he closed his eyes he could feel the warm flow of blood running over his fingers. But the best part was the look in Gus Thompson's eyes when the man realized he was going to die—and with his own knife.

The fool had gone for a knife in his boot after his gun had been taken away from him. It had been too easy to cut his throat. True, killing him had been a risky thing to do, especially killing him in the barn loft. But the dried hay would make it hard for forensics to find anything. Not to mention all the people who had tromped through that place.

He was reasonably sure he'd pulled it off without a hitch. He'd wiped off most of the blood on his hand in the hay, having cut the man's throat from behind him. Then he had slipped out of the barn to wash his hands in the hose on the back side of the barn.

He'd been careful not to leave any footprints next to the faucet. The police would suspect that he had to clean up. The creek would probably be their first choice, the hose behind the barn too obvious.

Either way, he'd managed to clean himself up and leisurely walk back to the house without causing anyone to take note of him.

All in all, it had been an amazing day. He felt better about everything. Now all he had to do was finish McKenzie Sheldon and life would be back to normal. Well, as normal as his life could be, under the circumstances.

But he was in no hurry. Killing Gus Thompson had filled his growing need. Now he could just relax and watch McKenzie sweat. With her former salesman's death, she would be terrified. He chuckled. And her cowboy would realize he was no match for him.

Soon he would call and ask to see a house. He knew exactly which one he would want to see. When he'd gotten home from the open house, he'd searched the paper and internet for a listing in the area that would work to his advantage.

As he picked up her card and ran his fingers over the dark engraving, he had no doubt that Ms. McKenzie Sheldon would accommodate him in every way possible.

Chapter Twelve

Dana met them at the ranch house door. "I am so glad you decided to come back."

McKenzie couldn't help being touched by the warm welcome, but she still had misgivings about being here. It must have showed in her face because Dana hugged her and said, "I have something I want to show you in the kitchen," leaving the men in the living room. Because it was late, the children were already in bed. The large, two-story ranch house was quieter than McKenzie had ever heard it.

"I know that you didn't want to come here," Dana said, the moment the kitchen door closed behind them.

"Only because there is a killer after me. I couldn't bear it if I brought my troubles here and put your family in danger."

"We've had our share of trouble at this ranch, believe me, and I'm sure we will again," Dana said. "For me this place has always been a sanctuary. If it can be for others..." She smiled and took McKenzie's hands in her own. "Then I'm glad. My mother loved this ranch, fought for it. It's that Old West spirit that lives here in this canyon. Hayes did right bringing you back here."

McKenzie wasn't as sure of that. But she had to admit, she felt safer here and more at home than she did even in her condo as the two of them joined the men.

"We're going down to the Corral tonight," Dana said as if the idea had just come to her. "You dance, don't you, McKenzie?"

She started to shake her head.

"Not to worry," Hayes said. "I'll teach you Texas two-step."

"It's Saturday night in the canyon," Tag said. "You really do not want to miss this. Isn't that right, Lily?" His fiancée laughed and agreed.

McKenzie couldn't help but get caught up in their excitement. "Saturday night in the canyon. How can I say no?"

Hayes smiled at her. "It's going to be fun, I promise."

She didn't doubt it. The Cardwells were a family that had fun; she could see that. She found herself smiling as they all piled into a couple of rigs and drove up the canyon to the Corral Bar.

"I forgot to mention that my father and uncle are playing in the band," Dana said as they got out.

McKenzie could hear the music, old-time country, as they pushed through the door. The place was packed, but Hayes pulled her out onto a small space on the dance floor, anyway.

The song was slow, a mournful love song. He took her in his arms, drawing her close. She'd danced some in her younger days, mostly with her sisters, though.

Hayes was easy to follow and she found herself relaxing in his arms and moving with the music.

"You're a fast learner," he whispered next to her ear, making her smile.

They danced the next couple of songs, the beat picking up.

"Are you having fun?" Hayes asked.

She was. She laughed and nodded as he spun her, catching her by the waist to draw her back to him. She loved being in his arms and it wasn't just because she felt safe there. She was falling for Hayes Cardwell.

"Here, you need this after that last dance," Tag said, handing each of them a beer as they came off the dance floor. "Some nice moves out there, little brother." He winked at Hayes. "Who knew he could dance?"

"He is a man of many talents," McKenzie agreed as she tried to catch her breath. Just being around Hayes made her heart beat faster and her pulse sing. When he looked at her like he was doing now… "He just taught me the Texas swing."

"Come to Texas and I'll teach you all kinds of things," Hayes said, meeting her gaze and holding it.

She laughed that off but she could tell he was serious. Texas? She didn't think so. She hadn't spent years working her tail off to get her business where it was to pack up and move.

And yet when she looked into his dark eyes, she was tempted. She told herself it had only been an off-handed remark. They hardly knew each other. A woman would be crazy to pack up and move clear across country because of a man, wouldn't she?

HAYES COULD HAVE bitten his tongue. He'd seen his brother's surprised expression. He'd been joking. Or at least he thought he had when he'd started to suggest it. But by the time the words were out of his mouth…

He shook his head and took a long drink of his beer. From the moment he'd looked into McKenzie Sheldon's eyes he'd been spellbound. He couldn't explain it but the woman had cast a spell on him.

The band took a break and Dana and McKenzie headed off to the ladies' room together. He decided it was as good as any time to go over to say hello to his father and uncle.

"I heard you were in the canyon," his father said, giving him a slap on the back. Harlan Cardwell was still strong and handsome for a man in his sixties.

Tag had bonded with their father on his visit to Montana last Christmas. Hayes only had vague memories of occasional visits from his father while growing up.

"Good to see you," he said, then shook his uncle Angus's hand. The two had been playing in a band together, Tag had told him, since they were in high school.

"I've gotten to know Dad better," Tag had said when their father's name had come up. "He's a loner, kind of like Austin. He and his brother are close, but Uncle Angus doesn't even see his own daughter Dana that much."

"So you're saying our uncle is just as lousy a father as our own?" he'd asked Tag. "That's reassuring."

"I'm saying there's more to them. Dad cares, but neither he nor his brother, it seems, were cut out to be family men."

Several locals came up to talk to Harlan and Angus. Hayes told his father he would catch him later and went to find McKenzie.

Hayes had always wondered about his father. What man let his wife raise five boys alone? Not that their mother wasn't one strong woman who'd done a great job.

"That's your father?" McKenzie asked, studying the elderly cowboy.

"That's him." Hayes had only recently learned that his father and uncle had spent most of their lives working for various government agencies. Both were reportedly retired.

He didn't want to talk about his father. "About earlier when I suggested you come to Texas…"

"I might come down just to see what all the fuss is about sometime," she said and quickly added, "Just to visit."

Fortunately, the band broke into a song. McKenzie put down her beer and, taking her hand, he led her back out on the dance floor.

As he pulled her into his arms, though, he couldn't bear to think about the day he would have to go back to Texas without her.

"ARE YOU ALL RIGHT?" Hayes asked as they walked toward their cabins after they'd closed down the Corral. Tag had stayed behind to talk to Hud on the porch, while Dana had gone into the house to see how the kids were. Her sister Stacy had come up from Bozeman to watch all the kids for them.

The night was cool and dark in the pines. Only the starlight and a sliver of white moon overhead lit their way through the dense trees. In the distance, McKenzie thought she could hear the river as it wound through the canyon. It reminded her of the music back at the bar and being in Hayes's arms.

"I'm fine," she said and breathed in the sweet summer night's scents, wishing this night would never have to end.

He took her hand, his fingers closing around hers, and instinctively she moved closer, their shoulders brushing.

"I enjoyed visiting with your father tonight. He seems sweet." She glanced over at Hayes. "He said he wants to get to know his sons. I can tell he's sorry he missed so many years with the five of you." She saw that it was a subject he didn't want to talk about. There was hurt there. She wondered what it would take to heal it. With Hayes in Houston and his father here, well, that was too many miles, too much distance between them in more ways than one.

"I had a great time tonight," she said, changing the subject. She didn't want anything to ruin this night. She felt still caught up in the summer night's festivities. If anything, she had fallen even harder for the Cardwell family tonight.

"Me, too. So you aren't sorry I brought you here?"

She laughed as she looked at him. He wore his gray Stetson, his face in shadow, but she knew that face so well now that she knew he was pleased she'd had fun.

"I'd rather be here with you than anywhere else in the world tonight."

He squeezed her hand then drew her to a stop in the pines just yards from her cabin. A breeze swayed the boughs around them, whispering softly, as he pulled her to him. The kiss was warm and soft and sweeter than even the night.

"McKenzie, that isn't just the beer talking, is it?" he joked.

She cupped his face in her hands, drawing him down to her lips. All night she'd wanted his arms around her. All night she'd wanted him. As she put into the kiss the longing she had for him, he dragged her against him with a groan. Desire shot through her blood, hot and demanding.

When she finally drew back, she whispered on a ragged breath, "I want you, too, Hayes Cardwell, and that isn't the beer talking."

They were so close she could see the shine of his dark eyes in the starlight. Without another word, he swept her up in his arms and carried her into the cabin.

As the cabin door closed behind them, Hayes lowered McKenzie slowly to her feet. His need for her was so strong that he would have taken her right there on the floor. But not their first time, he told himself as he looked into her eyes, losing himself in the clear blue sea.

"Last chance," he said quietly.

"Not a chance."

She started to unbutton her blouse, but he stopped her, moving her hands away to do it himself. He was determined to take it slow. As he slipped one button free, then another, he held her gaze. Her blouse fell open. He slowly lowered his eyes to her white-laced bra against the olive of her skin.

He brushed his fingertips over the rise of her breasts. She moaned softly as he dipped into the bra. Her nipple hardened under his thumb, making her arch against his hand. Her skin felt as hot as his desire for her. He released the front snap of her bra, exposing both breasts. Need burned through him, making him ache.

He'd wanted her for so long. When his gaze returned to her face, he saw her own need in her eyes. In one swift movement, she unsnapped his shirt, making the snaps sing. She pressed her palms to his chest.

He felt heat race along his nerve endings. He bent to kiss her then drew her against him, feeling her full breasts and hard nipples warm his skin and send his growing desire for her rocketing.

His mouth dropped to her breast, his tongue working the nipple. His hand slipped up under her skirt and her panties. She arched against him, rocking against his hand until she cried out and sagged against him.

He unhooked her skirt. It dropped to the floor. Her white lace panties followed it. Naked, she was more beautiful than he could have imagined. He swung her up in his arms again and carried her into the bedroom. As he started to lower her on the bed, she pulled him down into a hot, deep kiss and then her hand was on the buttons of his fly.

Lost in the feel of her, he made love to her slow and sweet, but it took all of his effort to hold back. The second time, he didn't hold back. They rolled around on the bed, caught up in a passion that left them both spent.

Later, as they lay on the bed staring up at the skylight overhead and trying to catch their breath, he looked over at McKenzie. She was smiling.

PATIENCE. HE KNEW things would be hot for a while with the cops, which meant there was no going near McKenzie's condo or office. Killing Gus came at a cost. Now he had to live with the consequences.

Tonight he sat on his porch considering his options. One would be to go back to work. It would look better should he find himself on the suspect list. Anyone who'd been to the open houses would be scrutinized. He wasn't worried. He looked great on paper.

Gus hadn't told the police anything—just as he'd sworn before he died. He'd had to make sure the police didn't have the license plate number of the van he'd been driving that night outside McKenzie's condo. Gus hadn't given the police even the make of the vehicle he'd been driving. He couldn't believe his luck—or Gus Thompson's stupidity. Gus was the only one who could have identified him and now he was dead.

Luck was with him. It buoyed him in this difficult time. He could last a couple of days without seeing McKenzie, without going near her. Unless there was another way.

The idea came to him slowly, teasing him in its simplicity. The only way he could get to McKenzie Sheldon sooner would be if her attacker were caught. He thought of the men he'd seen at the open house. A couple of them had looked familiar. In fact, there was one he knew. He was the right size. All it would take was a couple of pieces of incriminating evidence to be found at the man's house. The police would think they had their man.

So would McKenzie Sheldon.

There would be no reason for her not to go back to work as usual.

He felt good as he got up and went to bed. When he closed his eyes, he relived every moment from the time he hit Gus Thompson and knocked him to his knees until he saw the life drain out of the man. It had been a good day.

But he couldn't stop himself from dreaming about the day he would take McKenzie Sheldon for his own. Normally, he only spent a few hours with each one. Too much time increased the chance of being caught.

With McKenzie, though, he wanted to take his time. He would have to find some place where they could be alone for more than a few hours.

MCKENZIE LAY IN the bed, the stars glittering like tiny white lights through the skylight overhead, Hayes Cardwell lying next to her.

"So I have to know," McKenzie said, rolling up on one elbow to look at him. "What makes good Texas barbecue?"

Hayes smiled over at her. "Are you serious?"

"Come on. You can tell me your secret. Isn't that how you and your brothers got your start? It has to be some kind of special barbecue."

He nodded as he rolled up on his side to face her.

"You have to understand. We were raised on barbecue." He closed his eyes for a moment and sniffed as if he could smell it. "You've got to have the smoke," he said as he opened his eyes and grinned at her. "And that takes a pit and a lot of patience. Most people don't know this, but cooking whole animals over smoldering coals is thought to have originated in the Caribbean. The Spanish saw how it was done and called it barbacoa. It's been refined since then, of course, and every region does it differently. Texas is known for its brisket, cooked charred black and bursting with flavor."

She laughed. "What makes your brisket so special?"

"We cover them with special seasonings and then smoke them for twelve to eighteen hours in wood-burning pits."

"Secret seasonings, right?"

"You better believe it. But wait until you taste our barbecue sauce."

"I can't wait. Am I going to get a chance to taste it?"

"Count on it," Hayes said and kissed her. It was a slow, sexy kiss that sent a throbbing ache of desire through her. She knew it wouldn't take much to find herself making love with him again. He'd been so tender the first time. The second time he'd taken her in a way that still had her heart pounding.

Just the thought brought with it the remembered pleasure. But as intimate as their lovemaking had been, she needed to know more about this man. She'd put her life into his hands. She felt as if he had done the same.

"I heard you started with just one small restaurant," she said.

He nodded. "We opened the first place in an old house with the pit out back. It was just good ol' traditional barbecue like we grew up on. You can take a cheap piece of meat and, if you cook it properly and with the right wood, it becomes a delicacy. One whiff and I can tell whether hickory, post oak or mesquite was used. But in the end, give me a piece of marbled pork shoulder and I will make you a tender, succulent pulled pork sandwich like none you've ever had before. The secret is that you've got to have smoky pork fat."

She smiled at him, hearing the pride in his voice. "Coleslaw?"

"Of course. You have to slather some sweet slaw on the pulled pork along with our spicy barbecue sauce to cut the richness of the pork. We also do a mean Southern potato salad and you are not going to believe our beans."

She had to laugh. "You're making me hungry."

"Me, too." His gaze locked with hers, making it clear it wasn't just barbecue he was hungry for.

"So the business just took off."

He nodded, almost sheepishly, as if embarrassed by their success. "None of us saw that coming."

Just like they hadn't seen this coming, she thought as Hayes kissed her. This time she let nature take its course. She couldn't bear the thought, though, that with a killer after her, this could be the last time they made love.

"WHAT'S GOING ON, HAYES?" Tag demanded.

Hayes started as his brother stepped out of the trees

next to his cabin a few hours before daylight. He was surprised and more than a little irritated. "Have you been waiting for me this whole time?"

"Don't try to avoid the question. What's the deal with you and McKenzie Sheldon?"

Hayes thought about telling him it was none of his business. But since the five brothers had been little, they'd taken care of each other. He knew his brother was asking out of concern, not idle curiosity.

"I don't know."

"This is moving a little fast, don't you think?" his brother asked.

"Oh, you're a good one to talk, Tag. You come up here for Christmas and the next thing we know, you're engaged to be married and want us to open a barbecue joint up here."

"I fell in *love.* It happens and sometimes, it happens fast." Tag studied him for a moment. "Are you telling me that's what's happening to you?"

Hayes looked out at the mountains, now dark as the pines that covered them, then up at the amazing big sky twinkling with stars. Had he ever seen a clearer sky—even in Texas?

"What if I am falling in love with her?" he demanded.

Tag laughed and shook his head. "The Cardwells just can't do anything the easy way, can they? Bro, there is a killer after her and probably after you, as well, now."

"Don't you think I know that? I have to find him before..." He pulled off his hat and raked his fingers through his hair. "I have to find him."

"Okay, and then what?"

Hayes met his brother's gaze. "I don't know. I think about Jackson and his marriage—"

"It doesn't have to end up that way," Tag said as he followed him into the cabin. "Jackson was blinded by first love. He didn't see that all she really wanted was his money. Does McKenzie Sheldon want your money?"

"No." He let out a chuckle. "I'm not even sure she wants me for the long haul."

It was Tag's turn to laugh. "I've seen the way she looks at you. You're her hero."

"Yeah. That's what bothers me. I'm no hero. What happens when she realizes that? Worse, what if I get her killed?"

Chapter Thirteen

Hayes looked toward the house where McKenzie and Dana had just disappeared inside.

"Sorry I came down on you like I did last night," Tag said. "It's none of my business."

In the clear light of day, Hayes now understood why his brother had been so upset with him the night before. "Last night shouldn't have happened. It's all my fault. I should never have let it go as far as it did. My life is in Texas."

"Shouldn't you be telling her this instead of me?" his brother asked.

Hayes barely heard him. "Her life is here. She's spent these years building up a business she is proud of. I couldn't ask her to give that up. Not that I would. Not that things have gone that far."

"Take it easy, bro. You made love to her. You didn't sign away your life in blood."

"I take making love seriously."

Tag laughed. "We all do."

"You know what I mean."

"Did you tell her you loved her?"

"Of course not."

"Because you don't?"

"No, because we barely know each other. I don't even know how she feels or how I do, for that matter."

Tag shook his head. "You're falling for this woman."

He could see Dana and McKenzie inside the house. They seemed to be having a heart-to-heart. He could almost feel his ears burn just thinking what McKenzie might be telling his cousin about last night.

"If you care about her, you should tell her," Tag said. "It sounds to me like you need to figure out how you feel about her."

"It's complicated."

"It always is," Tag said. "But God forbid if anything happens to her, you'll never forgive yourself if you don't tell her."

DANA HAD PACKED them a picnic lunch and offered to help saddle horses for the ride up the mountain to the lake. "It's beautiful up there. Crystal clear and surrounded by large boulders. There is one wonderful rock that is huge and flat on top. Have your picnic up there. Or there is a lovely spot in the pines at the edge of the water. I think that is my favorite."

McKenzie gave Dana a hug. "Thank you."

"My pleasure." She smiled as she looked out the window to where her two Cardwell cousins were standing by the corral after a huge Montana breakfast of chicken-fried venison steaks, hash browns, biscuits with milk gravy and eggs peppered with fresh jalapeños from Dana's garden.

Tag was handsome as sin, but nothing like Hayes, McKenzie was thinking.

"He's special, isn't he?"

She gave a start, but didn't have to ask who she was referring to.

"Hayes reminds me of Hud." Dana met her gaze. "He's a keeper."

"His life is in Houston."

"So was Tag's," she pointed out with a grin. "It wouldn't hurt to have two Cardwell cousins up here, making sure this barbecue restaurant is a success. Wouldn't hurt to have a private-investigative business here, either."

"You're a shameless matchmaker," McKenzie joked.

"Just like my mother. Did I tell you that she made a new will before she died, leaving me the ranch? Unfortunately, she was killed in a horseback-riding accident and no one could find the will. I almost lost the ranch. If Hud and I hadn't gotten together again I would have never found the will and been able to keep this place."

"Where was the will?"

"In my mother's old recipe book marking the page with Hud's favorite cookie recipe," Dana said and laughed. "Love saved this ranch."

McKenzie had to laugh, as well. The more she was around Dana Cardwell Savage, the more she found herself wanting to be a part of this amazing family. For a few moments, she could even forget that there was a killer after her.

THE HIGH MOUNTAIN lake was just as beautiful as Dana had said it would be, Hayes thought as he swung down off his horse.

"It's breathtaking," McKenzie said as she dismounted and walked to the edge of the deep green pool.

"*You're* breathtaking," Hayes said behind her.

She smiled at him over her shoulder, then bent down and scooped up the icy water to toss back at him. He'd told himself that last night had been a mistake, that he wouldn't let it happen again. But right now all he could think about was McKenzie being in his arms again.

The droplets felt good, even though he jumped back, laughing. He loved seeing her like this, relaxed and carefree as if she didn't have a care in the world. He doubted she'd ever been like this—even before the attack. The woman had been driven in a single-minded determination to succeed. He couldn't help but wonder if any of that mattered now. Was it the attack that had changed her? Or could it possibly be that she had feelings for him? Long-lasting feelings?

He'd spent the morning on the phone with the police and doing some investigating online. The police had run the license plates of those who had attended, but with Gus Thompson's murder, they weren't giving out any information. All they'd told him was that they were checking into everyone who'd been there both for the attack on McKenzie *and* Gus Thompson's murder.

Hayes had run checks on the two men who had provided McKenzie with their names.

Would her attacker be so brazen as to give her his real name, though?

The first name he ran was Bob Garwood. The man had a military background, special ops, and had received a variety of medals before being honorably discharged.

If anything, it showed that he had special training, something that could be an advantage for a man who abducted women and killed them.

Bob Garwood had no record, not even a speeding ticket. He looked clean. Maybe McKenzie was right and he *had* been merely looking for a date the two times he'd come to her open houses.

Or maybe not, Hayes thought, as he saw that Bob Garwood owned a gym-equipment business. Did that mean he traveled? Hayes bet it did. The company he owned was called Futuristic Fitness, promising to sell the most up-to-the-moment, technologically advanced equipment on the market. That could explain why the man was in such good shape.

The next name he ran was Jason Mathews. He was an antiquities appraiser, another job where he no doubt traveled. Like Bob Garwood, Jason Mathews looked clean. He was married, owned his house and volunteered for several charitable organizations—not that any of that cleared him, Hayes thought, reminded of Gacy who dressed as a clown at charitable functions.

The police hadn't found anything suspicious about

any of the other viewers who'd attended the open house from what he'd been told. They were still investigating.

Hayes had finally given up in frustration. He couldn't even be sure that McKenzie's attacker had driven to the open house. He could have come by foot; in fact, that seemed more likely since when he stumbled upon Gus Thompson, he hadn't hesitated to kill him, even though it was a dangerous thing to do.

"I guess swimming is out," McKenzie said wistfully.

"Not necessarily," Hayes answered as he began to pull off his boots. He could use a cold dip in the lake. Not that he thought it would help. "Dana packed towels as well as a blanket." He raised a brow and McKenzie laughed as she hurriedly began to undress.

"Last one in has to unpack the lunch."

THE CALL CAME forty-eight hours later. The police had received an anonymous tip from a neighbor. When they'd gone to a man by the name of Eric Winters's house to talk to him, they'd spotted incriminating evidence in his car and gotten a search warrant. Inside the house, they'd found the knife believed used to kill Gus Thompson along with items believed to have belonged to female victims that he'd kept as souvenirs—including McKenzie's red, high-heeled shoe.

McKenzie began to cry when she got the news as she thought of his other victims. The name Eric Winters meant nothing to her. Even when the police described the man to her, she couldn't place him, but apparently he'd come through the open house for the ranchette.

He'd just been one of a dozen men who could have been her attacker.

"So it's definitely him?" she asked, weak with relief.

"Given the evidence we found at his house, we have the man who attacked you. Your shoe will have to be kept as evidence."

"It's all right. I won't be wearing those heels again, anyway. Thank you so much for letting me know." For so long she'd thought they would never find him, that she would always be looking over her shoulder. She hung up and turned to look at Hayes. Her eyes welled again with tears as she said, "They got him," and stepped into Hayes's arms.

Dana threw a celebratory dinner complete with champagne that night. "Stay," she pleaded when McKenzie thanked her for everything and told her she would be moving out of the cabin in the morning.

"I wish I could stay. I love it up here, but I have a business to run. I've been away from it for too long as it is." The business had been her world just a week ago. It had taken all of her time and energy as well as her every waking thought. Until Hayes, she hadn't realized what she was missing.

But now he had no reason to stay and she had no reason not to return to her life, even if it did suddenly feel empty.

"And Hayes?" Dana asked, as if sensing her mood.

McKenzie looked across the room where the men were gathered. "I guess there is nothing keeping him in Montana now," she said.

Dana lifted an eyebrow in response. "You could ask

him to stay… Otherwise, he'll be back next month for Tag's wedding…."

McKenzie smiled at her new friend. "He *has* asked me to be his date."

Dana grinned knowingly. "That's if he can stay away from you until the wedding. I guess we'll see."

"I guess we will," she agreed. The thought of the wedding buoyed her spirits a little, but there was no denying it. Things had changed. *She* had changed. While she had to get back to work, it wasn't with the same excited expectation that she usually felt at the prospect. True, she would never feel as safe as she had, not in Bozeman, not in her condo. But it was more than that.

She'd fallen for the man, for his family, for even this ranch lifestyle. Not that she was about to admit that to him or his cousin, for that matter. As she'd told Dana, Hayes had a life in Houston. She had a life here. He hadn't asked to get involved. He hadn't even wanted her to know he was the one who'd saved her that night, she reminded herself.

As Hayes turned to look at her, he smiled and she felt her heart rise up like a bubble. She smiled back, fighting tears.

WHERE WAS SHE?

The words had been rattling around in his brain for four days now. It had taken the police several days to arrest Eric Winters. But now two more days had passed. Hadn't the police told her that her attacker had been caught? What was she waiting for? She should be back at work—and so should he. He couldn't afford to take much more time off. As it was, people were starting to notice. He couldn't keep saying he was taking off time to look for another house.

Unfortunately, his Realtor had disappeared. He'd expected her to hide out for a while after poor Gus Thompson's death. But that was almost a week ago. She hadn't been staying at her condo. Nor had she been going to her office. When he'd called the office, he'd been told that she couldn't be reached. He'd declined another real-estate agent, saying he had talked to Ms. Sheldon and only she could answer his questions.

From the exasperated tone of the receptionist's voice, he gathered that he wasn't the only one trying to reach her. Like him, surely she couldn't be away from work too long. Not a woman like her. She must be champing at the bit to return. These days away must be driving her insane.

Her absence was certainly pushing him over the edge. He didn't know how much longer he could stand it. He had to find her and finish this.

His instincts told him that she was with the cowboy. Before he'd killed Gus Thompson, he'd found out that the cowboy's name was Hayes Cardwell and that he was from Houston, Texas. He was considering opening a restaurant at Big Sky.

Cardwell. Wasn't there a ranch up there by that name? That had to be where McKenzie Sheldon was hiding. It would be too dangerous to go to the ranch. No, he had to find another way to flush her out.

He picked up the phone and called her office. He'd been careful not to come on too strong with the receptionist. He hadn't wanted to call too much attention to himself. But this time— "M.K. Realty, may I help you?"

"I sure hope so. I've been hoping to reach Ms. Sheldon, but now another house with another Realtor has come up—"

"I would be happy to put you through to her—"

"I've already left messages for her."

"Ms. Sheldon is at her desk this morning. I'll put you right through. May I say who's calling?"

HAYES LOOKED OUT the office window at the Houston skyscape. Just hours ago he'd been in the Gallatin Valley looking out at the mountains as his plane banked and headed south. Now here, he couldn't believe there had ever been a time that this had felt like home.

"What's bothering you?" Laramie demanded behind him from his desk. "If you still have doubts about opening a restaurant in Montana—"

"It's not that," he said, turning away from the view. The offices for Texas Boys Barbecue had started out in a corner of an old house not all that long ago. Now, though, it resided in a high-rise downtown with other corporations that pulled in millions of dollars a year.

"What is it, then?" Laramie demanded. "You've been acting oddly since you walked into my office."

"It's nothing." He didn't want to talk about McKenzie. It only made it harder. Better to put her and Montana behind him. "Have you talked to Austin?"

"You really want to talk about Austin?" his brother asked as Hayes took a seat across from him. "I've never seen you mope around over a woman before."

"I'm not—"

"Have you talked to her?"

Hayes gave up denying his mood had nothing to do with McKenzie. "She sounds like she is back at work and doing fine."

"And you probably told her you are back at work, too, and doing fine, right?"

He made a face at his brother. "She's happy with her life."

"Is that what she told you? Hayes, do you know anything about women?"

He had to laugh. "Not really. But I'm not sure you're the man to give me advice. Have you dated a woman more than once?"

"Very funny. One of you has to say it."

"Say what?"

Laramie groaned. "That you're in love. That is the problem, you know. You've fallen for the woman." He raised a hand. "Don't even bother to deny it. The question now is what are you going to do about it? Mope around and feel sorry for yourself or go get your woman?"

Hayes started to tell him how off base he was, but he saved his breath. "Just fly up there and go riding in on my white horse? Then what? I have a house, an office and a job here in Houston."

"Are you serious? You would let a simple stumbling block like those things keep you from what you really want? What did you do with my brother Hayes who has always gone after what he wants?"

"I've just never wanted anything this badly and I

don't even know if I can have her," he admitted and not easily.

"Only one way to find out. Better saddle up and get yourself back to Montana." Laramie picked up the phone. "Take the corporate jet. I'll have the pilot standing by."

"Ms. Sheldon?" He couldn't believe she was actually in her office, actually on the other end of the line. "I'm so glad to catch you in your office."

He'd been following the story about Eric Winters in the newspaper and on the evening television news. The man hadn't even been able to get out on bail. And now they were saying he could be a serial killer, having abducted and killed women all across the West. McKenzie must feel so safe, believing her attacker was finally behind bars.

"My wife and I are interested in seeing one of your houses. I was hoping you would be able to show us the residence as soon as possible. My wife was very impressed by you when we met you a while back. I told her I would see if you were free to show the house yourself. I know you own M.K. Realty." He'd learned that acknowledging that he knew who he was dealing with often worked.

"When were you thinking of seeing the house?" she asked, even though he could tell she had been ready to give him to someone else at the agency.

"My wife is very anxious. She doesn't want this house to get snatched up by someone else. I would imagine that now is too soon?" He heard her surprise.

Before she could draw a breath, he said, "It's the one you have listed as executive, high-end home with a million-dollar view."

"I'm familiar with the house."

"I believe it also has a several-million-dollar price tag. I can't tell you what I would have to contend with if we lost it before my wife even got a chance to see it."

"We can't have that," she said and he knew he had her. "I suppose I could show the house in, say, an hour?"

"I really appreciate this. My wife and I will meet you out there, if that is all right." This was working out even better than he'd hoped.

"I look forward to it. I'm sorry. I didn't catch your name."

"It's Jason. Jason and Emily Mathews."

"Yes, I remember we met at several of my showings." She sounded uneasy and he knew he had to mention the murder.

"I was so sorry to hear about your colleague being killed. That was such a shock. I'm glad the murderer has been caught. You just don't expect that kind of thing in Montana."

"It's rare, fortunately," she said and quickly changed the subject. "I'll see you soon, then, Mr. Mathews."

"Please call me Jason."

Chapter Fourteen

The moment McKenzie got off the phone she walked over to one of the cubicles.

"Jennifer, would you be able to take one of my showings this afternoon?"

The real-estate agent looked up in surprise. McKenzie had never asked any of them to take her showings until this moment.

The woman blinked then said, "I'd be happy to. Are you not feeling well?"

McKenzie almost laughed. "It's just that I have one before it that could take a while. Also I don't want you going alone. See if Rafe can go with you. I've decided from now on, we won't be showing houses alone if at all possible, but definitely any that could run over after dark."

"But aren't you showing one now alone?" Jennifer asked tentatively.

"It will be all right this one time. I'm meeting a man and his wife at the Warner place."

"I'm sure Rafe can go with me."

"Great. Thanks for doing this." As she walked back

to her office, McKenzie felt relieved. She had the other showing covered and after today, she would start relying more on her staff. If being gone had taught her anything, it was that she was not indispensible. For so long, she'd thought she had to do everything herself and yet when she'd returned after being gone for a week, she found that the agency was doing just fine.

There'd been numerous calls for follow-ups on houses she'd shown, but her staff had taken care of all but a couple of them. One of those was probably Mr. and Mrs. Mathews. Jason Mathews came across as the kind of man who only dealt with the boss or owner. Well, she was taking care of that one now.

McKenzie felt as if a weight had been lifted off her shoulders and at the same time, she couldn't help feeling a little sad. She hadn't heard from Hayes other than a quick phone call from the airport after he'd landed in Houston.

She'd gotten an agency call she'd had to take so she'd been forced to cut the call with Hayes short. When she'd tried to call him back, she'd gotten his voice mail. She hadn't left a message. What was there to say?

He'd asked how it felt to be back at work. She'd lied and said, "Great."

She'd asked him if he was glad to be home. He'd said he was.

That pretty much covered anything they had to say to each other, didn't it?

Outside her office, dark clouds had moved in. Thunder rumbled in the distance. The weatherman had warned that they might get some summer storms over the next few days.

Packing up her things, she headed for the door, also surprising her staff. She was always the first one in the office and the last to leave. As she walked out to her car in daylight, she couldn't help thinking of Hayes and Cardwell Ranch.

Was Hayes missing it and her as much as she was him? She pushed the thought away. She'd see him next month for Tag's wedding. The thought lightened her step even when it began to rain.

HE WAS WAITING for her. Anticipation had his heart racing. He'd failed once. He couldn't let that happen again.

Arriving early, he'd waited and gone over all the things that could go wrong. She might see that he hadn't brought his wife and panic, taking off before he could stop her. Or she might send someone else. Maybe even more possible, she might bring an associate.

He just couldn't let anything happen that would allow her to get away. Again.

He'd taken even more precautions since his failure with her the first time. He'd secured a place for them nearby. He couldn't chance transporting her any distance. Knowing Ms. Sheldon the way he did, she would be one of those women who got loose in the trunk, broke out a taillight and signaled for help.

Another precaution he was taking was knocking her out quickly. He'd opted to use a drug. He couldn't take the chance he might hit her too hard and kill her before all the fun began. It felt like cheating, drugging her, but he'd lost her once. That wasn't going to happen again. That's why he'd carefully chosen this huge monster of a house in the middle of the valley—and the abandoned house through the trees, only a short walk away.

Normally, he just dragged them out into the woods. But McKenzie Sheldon wasn't getting his quick and dirty usual fare. No, she was going to get the full treatment and that meant he would need a room inside a house.

He'd found one near the house he'd told her he wanted to view. He was counting on her not telling anyone where she was going. He was counting on it, based on the fact that she was the boss and that she would no longer be afraid since as far as she knew, her attacker was still behind bars.

The hard part would be getting her away from this house quickly and to their private spot. He would have to act fast, taking her in her car then coming back for his own car.

At the sound of a vehicle approaching, he tensed. McKenzie Sheldon was right on time. He checked the syringe in his pocket. Now, if she was alone, then nothing could stop him. He carefully adjusted the large straw hat balanced on the back of the passenger seat. From a distance it would appear his wife was sitting in the car waiting.

He glanced in his rearview mirror. It was McKenzie and she was alone. He smiled excitedly as he opened his car door and stepped out. All he needed was a few precious seconds and she'd be his.

HAYES THOUGHT ABOUT what his brother had said on the flight to Montana in the corporate jet. He also thought about McKenzie Sheldon's well-ordered life.

Like him, his career had taken up the greater part of his life. But that, he realized now, was because there hadn't been anything else that had interested him.

Now, his career, as important as it was, wasn't the first thing he thought of when he awakened in the morning. But was that true of McKenzie?

He'd seen her checking the messages on her phone, especially after a few days at the ranch. She'd been worried about her business. Not that he could blame her. She'd been such a major part of the agency he doubted she thought it could survive without her.

Hayes called McKenzie's office the moment the jet touched down outside of Bozeman, but was told she'd left work early.

"Have you tried her home?" the receptionist asked when he gave her his name. Word must have gone around the office that she'd spent almost a week with him up the canyon at Cardwell Ranch.

"She's already gone home?"

The receptionist laughed at his surprise. "I know it isn't like her. She even asked one of the associates to show a house for her this afternoon. We all thought she might have a date or something."

A date? He heard the woman try to swallow back her words.

"I mean we thought she was going out with you." Another gulp. "Is there a message I can give her if I hear from her?"

"No." He'd disconnected, wondering what he was doing flying to Montana. A *date?*

Well, what do you expect? he asked himself. *It wasn't as if you asked her to wait for you or even told her how you felt.*

Still, he hadn't been gone *that* long.

He tried her cell but it went to voice mail. On impulse, he called the office back and asked to speak to the sales associate who McKenzie had gotten to cover for her.

"This is Jennifer Robinson."

Hayes introduced himself and asked if she knew whether or not McKenzie was showing a house.

"She is, the Warner place."

That was the McKenzie Sheldon he knew, he thought with a sigh of relief. "Can you tell me how to find the Warner place? If she just left, I might be able to catch her."

MCKENZIE SAW THE large, newer-model expensive car parked by the house as she came up the drive.

Jason Mathews got out as she approached. She remembered him from the open house where Gus was killed. For a moment, she almost drove on through the circular drive and left.

You have nothing to fear. Your attacker was caught. Not only that, he brought his wife, right? As she glanced to the passenger seat, she saw a large summer straw hat and remembered that Emily Mathews was a tiny woman. Relief washed over her.

For a moment, though, she was sorry she hadn't

brought another agent with her. Her heart just wasn't in this, even though the sale would mean a very large commission. This was one of a number of houses in this area that the bank was anxious to get sold after a rash of foreclosures.

Having two agents go on every showing wasn't the best use of manpower. Also, she knew the nonlist agent would complain about losing money. Still, she wanted her agents to be safe and she would have gladly shared the commission.

Shutting off the car, she turned toward the passenger seat to dig the house keys out of her purse. To her surprise, her car door opened. She turned, startled to find Jason Mathews standing next to her car.

"I appreciate you taking the time to do this today," he said.

She tried to find her voice as she told herself he was just being polite, opening her door like that. "Just let me get the keys."

As she picked them up, she gripped them like a knife. Hayes's words came back to her that keys weren't much of a weapon because by then the attacker would be too close. Women lost their advantage up close because they were often the weaker sex.

At that moment, she was sorry she'd given Hayes back the pistol she used to have in her purse. She still had the can of pepper spray, but it would be in the bottom of her purse, not easily accessible.

All these thoughts hit her in a matter of seconds before Jason Mathews said, "I'll get Emily. She is anxious to see this house. Great location since she likes the idea of no neighbors within view."

He stepped away from the car and McKenzie felt herself breathe again. She chastised herself as she climbed out, dragging her purse out after her.

As she headed toward the house, she saw that Mr. Mathews was leaning into the car talking to his wife. For a woman who was anxious to see the house, she certainly was taking her time getting out of the car.

McKenzie headed for the front door of the house, just assuming the two would follow. Whatever discussion was going on between them, she didn't want to eavesdrop.

When her cell phone rang, she stopped partway up the wide front steps to dig the phone out of her purse. Busy thinking about Mrs. Mathews and hoping this hadn't been a wild goose chase, she didn't bother to check to see who was calling. "Hello?"

"McKenzie Sheldon? This is Officer Pamela Donovan with the Bozeman Police Department. I don't want to alarm you."

Alarm her? Surprised, she didn't hear Jason Mathews come up behind her until she felt the needle he plunged into her neck.

HAYES'S RENTAL CAR was waiting for him with the map inside just as he had requested. The Warner place, as Jennifer had called it, was about five miles outside of town to the south.

That meant it was at least fifteen miles from the airport. The worst part was the traffic. While nothing like Houston's, he'd managed to hit the valley during the afternoon rush hour. Just his luck.

He'd left a message with both Jennifer and the receptionist to have McKenzie call him if they heard from her. That's why when his phone rang he thought it would be her.

He was thrown for a moment when he realized the female voice on the other end of the line was the policewoman who'd worked with McKenzie after her attack.

"Yes, I remember you, Ms. Donovan."

"I just tried to reach Ms. Sheldon."

It was the worry he heard in her voice. "Is there a problem?"

"I didn't want to alarm her, but there is some news about the man we arrested in her attack. It might not mean anything—"

"What is it?" he asked as he drove toward the Gallatin Range of mountains to the south.

"McKenzie Sheldon isn't with you, by any chance, is she?" the policewoman asked.

"No. I was just on my way to the house she's showing. Why?"

He heard her hesitate before she said, "I just tried to reach her. We were cut off."

Unconsciously, he found himself driving a little faster. "Why were you trying to reach her?" Again the pause. "Officer—"

"There is some question whether or not the man we have in jail for her attack is guilty," the deputy finally said. "I can't get into it, but the dates of the other abductions aren't adding up for him and there is some question about the evidence we found in his house."

His heart pounded. "The dates. They don't add up for him, but they do for someone else, someone who was at the open house where Gus Thompson was killed, right?"

"When we went to bring Jason Mathews in for questioning, his wife told us that he'd had to leave town for a few days."

Hayes swore under his breath. "I was told at McKenzie's office that she was showing a house to a husband and wife." He prayed that was true and that the man sans the wife wasn't Jason Mathews. "I'm on my way there now." He gave her the directions he'd been given.

"We'll have a patrol car there as soon as possible."

Disconnecting, he drove as if his life depended on it, all the time mentally kicking himself for ever leaving. Worse, for never telling McKenzie how he felt about her.

MCKENZIE WOKE TO darkness. She tried to open her eyes but her lids felt too heavy. For a moment she couldn't remember anything. She cracked an eyelid open as she attempted to move. Her hands were bound with duct tape at the wrists in front of her, her feet were bound at the ankles and she was strapped to a wheelchair.

A shot of adrenaline rocketed through her as memory came back in a wave of nausea. The prick of the needle, the horror of what was happening as she slumped against Jason Mathews, the fleeting glimpse of the empty car except for the carefully positioned summer straw hat on the back of the passenger seat.

She looked around, terrified to see where he'd brought her.

"Well, hello," Jason Mathews said from where he stood nearby. "Nice to have you back."

With relief she saw that she was still dressed, but that several of the buttons on her blouse were open. She shuddered at the thought of this man's hands on her as she lifted her gaze. The room was small. A walk-in closet or maybe a pantry. Were they still at the Warner house? She didn't think so, but all of these high-end houses had similar features.

Drugged, it took her a moment to realize he hadn't gagged her. She opened her mouth and tried to scream. The sound that came out was weak. She tried again, stopping only when he erupted into a fit of laughing.

"No one can hear you. There's no one around for miles. Not that I mind hearing you scream. I plan to make you scream a whole lot more before this day is over."

His smile curdled her stomach. She tried to fight down the terror that weakened her as much as the drug he'd given her. Her mind raced. Had she told anyone at the office where she'd gone? Yes, Jennifer. She'd told her she was meeting a husband and wife at the Warner place. Not that there would be reason for anyone to start looking for her for hours. More like days.

Her heart dropped at the thought as the man stepped in front of her, forcing her to raise her gaze to his.

"Finally, we are alone," he said, smiling. "I was worried it wasn't ever going to happen. We are going to have so much fun. Well, I am," he added with a laugh. "First

I want to show you the house. It is only polite, since you showed me several houses." He stepped behind her and, kicking off the wheelchair brake, propelled her out of the small room into a larger one.

She saw that she'd been right about the space he'd had her in being a walk-in closet, even though there were no shelves or rods on the walls yet.

"The master bedroom!" he announced with a flourish. "I haven't had time to decorate, or even get a bed, so we'll have to make due."

Dust coated the floor. She frowned, trying to make sense of where they were. Not in the Warner place. She'd shown it before and it had been clean, although empty for some time like a lot of other houses in the neighborhood this far out of town. Were they in one of those houses? Some had been abandoned by the contractors when they'd gone broke and the banks had been slow to move on selling them.

Her gaze stopped on a pile of items in the corner of the room. Terror turned her bones to mush at the sight of the duct tape, handcuffs, gag ball and an array of sex toys, including a whip.

She closed her eyes, dropping her head, unable to look. She couldn't let herself give in to this. She had to find a way to escape. This wasn't the way she was going to die, not in this dirty, abandoned house with this madman.

"You need to wake up," he said next to her ear.

She didn't open her eyes. She needed to get away from him. She needed a weapon. She needed even half a chance. She could still feel the drug in her bloodstream. It made her limbs feel lifeless, her reflexes slow.

While driven, she'd still always been a realist. No one was going to save her and she didn't see any way to save herself, bound the way she was. He'd done this before. He knew what he was doing. And since she'd gotten away from him once, he had made sure she wouldn't this time, she thought as she tested the tape on her wrists and ankles.

He was going to kill her.

But not until he hurt her. She had seen the cruel glimmer in his eyes as soon as she'd looked at him moments before. For whatever reason, he liked hurting women. It must make him feel superior, not that his reasons mattered.

"I must have given you too much of the drug," he said, sounding disappointed, even angry. "I don't want you to miss a minute of the fun so you are going to have to wake up."

She kept her eyes closed. Let him think it was the drug.

The slap made her eyes fly open and slammed her head back against the webbing on the wheelchair seat. His face was inches from her own now, his breath rank as he laughed.

"I thought that might bring you out of it," he said with another laugh, and stepped behind the chair again. "Pay attention or the next time, I'll have to do something much more painful to get your attention."

He wheeled her through a door and into the large master bath. Her heart stopped at the sight of a roll of plastic in the bathtub and several new blue tarps spread over the floor. "That's for later. I want to put that part off as long as possible this time. You deserve my best after what you've put me through."

She heard the underlying anger in his voice. It made her blood run cold. He planned to hurt her for as long as he could keep her alive. A sob caught in her chest. "Why?" she cried, hating to let him see how terrified she was.

He laughed as he shoved her into the bedroom again then whirled the wheelchair around to face him. The blade of a pair of scissors caught the light, shimmering in his hand. She gasped and tried to draw back as he moved in closer.

"Why?" he asked mockingly. "Because I can."

The knife blade cut through the tape holding her to the chair an instant before he stepped behind the wheelchair and unceremoniously dumped her into the middle of the master bedroom floor. The sound of the blade cutting through the tape reminded her of it cutting through her hair.

"Tour over," he said. "It's time for the fun to begin."

She looked up at him from the floor where she lay on her side, bound and helpless. If she couldn't get away, then there was only one thing to do. She had to make him so furious that he killed her quickly.

Chapter Fifteen

Hayes hit a rain shower near the mountains. It was still spitting rain as the Warner place came into view. The massive house sat on a small rise with a stand of aspens and pines behind it. From the third floor, he would guess there was a three-hundred-and-sixty-degree view of the valley. The house was just as Jennifer at the agency had described it. Massive, tan with matching stone and a circular driveway. The driveway was empty.

"No!" he yelled and slammed his fist against the steering wheel as he slowed. She couldn't have already come here, shown the house and left, unless… Once off the narrow paved road, the circular drive was an intricate pattern of cobblestones. Unfortunately, Montana winters had done their worst, breaking some and dislodging others. His tires rumbled over them as he neared the elaborate front door.

Unless the couple she was supposed to show the house to had called and canceled. He tried her number again. Again, it went straight to voice mail. Still, he was about to grasp onto that theory like a life raft when he saw the muddy footprints.

Hayes threw on the brakes. The rain had stopped. His windshield wipers scraped loudly across the dry glass. He shut them off, then leaving the rental running, got out.

The prints appeared to be muddy boot tracks. What had caught his eye was how they had trailed onto the cobblestones from the side of the house.

So she had shown the house to someone? He started to follow the tracks along the side of the house. The landscaping had never been finished except for a little out front. Peering in a window, he found the house was empty. It had that never-lived-in look and he was reminded of something McKenzie had told him about overbuilding back in the early two thousands. Building contractors had gone broke, leaving grandiose spec houses for the banks to deal with. This appeared to be one of them.

As he neared the back of the house, he expected the tracks to head for the rear entrance, assuming they must be from whomever McKenzie had shown the house to.

But the tracks veered off into the trees. Strange. The hair rose on the back of his neck as he realized the tracks had been heading out of the woods behind the house—and ended on the cobblestones out front.

What the hell? He'd put on his gun and shoulder holster after the call from the policewoman. He checked his gun now as he realized what he was seeing. Whoever had recently come to the Warner place from the trees hadn't walked back. They'd driven.

"DOES YOUR WIFE KNOW?"

He'd never let the others talk. He'd kept their mouths duct taped. He hadn't needed to hear their screams. The eyes were more than windows into the soul. He had been able to see their terror as their eyes widened in disbelief. None of them had been able to believe it was happening to them. When the realization that they were about to die finally hit them, it, too, was in their eyes. He hadn't needed to even hear more than their muffled screams.

"If Emily really is your wife, then she *must* know," McKenzie said. "No woman could be that stupid."

"Don't talk about my wife. She doesn't know anything," he snapped.

"She probably turns a blind eye, just thankful it isn't her."

"Emily isn't like that. She's sweet and kind and… If she knew…" His voice trailed off, the thought too horrifying. Emily loved him. She trusted him. She looked up to him. She wasn't like these successful bitches who looked down their noses at him. If only she had come along years ago before…the others.

"I bet she can smell it on you when you come home. Does she make you shower? Or does she like it, the smell of another woman's pain on you?"

"Enough!" he bellowed, his voice echoing in the cavernous empty room. "You don't know anything about it."

"Don't I? You know she can see it building up inside you, then you leave and when you come back…"

She met his gaze, hers hard as stone. "Believe me, she knows."

He kicked her, catching her in the stomach and flipping her over. A painful cry came out of her so he kicked her again, shutting her up except for the second groan of pain. He flipped her back over to face him as he dropped down beside her and cupped her face in his hands, pulling her a breath's distance from his own face.

"You want to know why I do this? Because of women like you. You think you're so smart. Bitches, all of you. But once you realize that you're mine to do with whatever I want, then you change your tune. Like the others, you will cry and whine and plead with me."

She spit in his face.

He screamed in fury, releasing her to slap her as hard as he could. Her head snapped back, smacking the floor. He hurriedly wiped her saliva from his face with his sleeve, cringing at the horrible feel of it on his skin. "I am going to kill you!" he yelled. "I'm going to—"

"Big man, killing a woman who is bound and helpless. This is what makes you feel better? If you were a real man—"

He snatched up the whip from the corner of the room and swung it at her. She tried to roll away from him, only managing to flip over once before the cat-tails sliced the back of her blouse open along with her skin. She screamed.

AS HAYES ENTERED the dark stand of trees, he pulled his weapon. Droplets from the rain still shone in the bright green leaves of the aspens and dripped down occasionally as he followed the tracks.

He hadn't gone far when the trees opened a little. He glimpsed the backyard of another house. Around him, everything was deathly quiet. He didn't even hear a birdsong, just the drip of the trees.

Hayes moved along the edge of the trees until he could see the front of the house. No vehicles and yet the tracks were fresh. Two sets. Both disappearing into the garage. His heart began to pound faster as he worked his way toward the back of the house, keeping out of sight of the rear windows.

He passed an old greenhouse, the door dangling open. Inside he would see where the vegetation had taken over, but rather than being green, everything appeared crusted with a thick layer of dust. It was the kind of thing that had creeped him out when he was a kid exploring old houses with his brothers.

He moved past the greenhouse and through an old garden spot, the dried cornstalks giving him cover until he was within a dozen yards of the back entrance to the house.

The muddy tracks ended on the back step. He drew out his phone and called 911. He was headed for the door when a scream pierced the silence.

The back door wasn't locked. That was because the man inside hadn't been expecting company? Or had set a trap for him? Hayes took a chance, slipping through and moving fast through the big, empty house.

He couldn't tell where the scream had come from, but there were tracks in the dust on the floor.

One set of man-sized footprints and two narrow wheel tracks. What the hell?

"NOT SO MOUTHY NOW, are you?" Jason said as he crouched down next to her.

The initial pain had been incredible. She'd never felt anything like it and could no more have held back the scream as she could have quit breathing.

Worse, she knew this was just the beginning. She could feel blood soaking into her blouse, running down her back.

He was kneeling next to her, his face close, so close she could feel his breath on her again. It took all her courage to look up into his face, knowing what she would find there. Satisfaction. He knew now that he could break her. There had probably never been a doubt in his mind. She was the fool for thinking she could trick this man into killing her.

He smiled. "I'm sorry. Did you have something else you wanted to say?"

As he started to move back from her, she swung her arms up, looping her bound wrists around his neck. She brought him down hard, pulling him off-balance and slamming his face into the floor next to her.

McKenzie knew it had been a stupid thing to do. She knew it wouldn't knock him out. If anything, it would only make him more furious and more determined to make her pay. She'd acted out of pain and fear and desperation.

He let out a bellow of pain and fury. She tried to slam his face down again, but he broke free of her hold, swinging wildly at her. She managed to roll away after only one blow, quickly rolling a second time so her back wasn't turned to him when he stumbled to his feet.

Dazed, his nose appearing broken and bleeding, he stared at her for a moment. He was breathing hard and looked unsteady on his feet. As he started toward her, she swung around on her butt and kicked him, knocking his feet out from under him.

He went down hard, hitting the wood floor with an *uhftt.* This time, he got up much faster and even as she tried to push herself back into the wall, he was on her, grabbing a handful of her short hair to drag her out into the center of the floor again.

"You have no idea what you've done!" he screeched at her as he held one hand to his bleeding nose and groped in his pocket with the other hand. Something silver flashed in his free hand an instant later.

McKenzie saw the scissors blade gleam in the late-afternoon light an instant before he lunged at her.

HAYES HADN'T GONE far into the house when he heard what sounded like a battle going on overhead. Of course, McKenzie would put up a fight just as she had the night she was attacked in the grocery-store parking lot, fighting for her life.

Rushing through the massive house, he finally found the stairs. What he saw brought him up short. There were no footprints in the dust on the steps and for an instant he stood confused, fighting to make sense of what he was seeing. He could hear sounds of a fight going on upstairs and yet—

That's when he spotted the elevator and the tracks leading into it—the same ones he'd found just inside the back door—a man's muddy boot prints and the two narrow wheel tracks.

He took off up the stairs at a dead run, weapon drawn. McKenzie's scream filled the air as he topped the stairs. He followed the sound, still running, breathing hard, knowing he would kill the man. Blinded with rage, he wanted to tear the man limb from limb. Hayes had never felt that kind of anger. It scared him and yet it also fueled him as he ran toward the heartbreaking sounds. He just prayed he would reach McKenzie before the madman killed *her.*

AS JASON MATHEWS lunged at her with scissors, he let out a roar. She caught a glimpse of the insanity burning in his eyes. He came at her like a wounded animal, only this animal didn't just want to fight back. This animal yearned for retribution as only a human animal can.

He came at her so fast, she didn't get a chance to swing around with her feet. He came at her face, slashing the blades wildly. Had he simply tried to stab her, she might not have raised her hands to protect herself. But then again, she might have instinctively. She would never know.

She felt the blades slash across the backside of one wrist where she was bound by the thick tape. Because of that, she didn't feel the pain at first. She'd drawn her feet up as he'd struck her and managed to kick out at him, catching him in one knee. She heard screaming and thought at first it was her.

His leg buckled and he came down on top of her. She tried to roll out from under him, but he was too heavy. He had her pinned to the floor as he tried to struggle to his feet.

He rose just enough that he could get the scissors between them. He was going to kill her. Not the way he had wanted. But he could no longer hold back. She saw it in his expression as he struggled to rise.

Defeat, it was in his eyes, as well as disgust and pain. His nose was still bleeding and there was a bruised spot on his forehead from where it must have connected to the floor. The bright red blood had run down onto his white shirt.

How would he explain that to his wife?

That crazed, terrified thought came out of nowhere. The random thought of a woman about to die.

Hayes. The thought of him came with such regret she felt tears well in her eyes. She didn't want to die without at least telling him that she'd fallen in love with him.

Jason steadied himself as he timed his next thrust, this one aimed at her heart. They were both breathing hard, his breath making a loud almost snoring sound because of his broken nose. Neither of them heard the pounding of footfalls in the hallway.

Jason raised the scissors, meeting her gaze with one of rage and pain. He looked as if he was about to cry. McKenzie wanted to look away, but she couldn't. Her eyes locked with his. He almost looked afraid of her. He just wanted it to be over, she thought and realized that killing her this way wouldn't give him what he needed so there would be other women—and soon. That thought filled her with more sorrow than the thought of her own imminent death.

With the look of a man about to drive a stake into a vampire's heart, he grabbed the scissors in both hands and brought the blades down.

The sound of the gunshot was like an explosion, even in the large master suite. Another shot filled the air. Then another and another.

McKenzie had accepted that she would die. She'd told herself not to fight it as Jason drove the scissor blades down at her heart. But the gunshots into his back threw off his aim and gave her a few seconds to shift her body to the side. The blades came down into her side in a searing pain. Her cry was lost in the echo of the gunshots.

HAYES THOUGHT OF the first time he'd laid eyes on McKenzie Sheldon. She'd been lying on the ground bleeding and then her eyes had opened....

He shoved the madman's body off her and dropped to his knees next to her.

"McKenzie!" There was blood everywhere. He couldn't tell how much of it was hers as he felt for a pulse, praying with every second that he would feel one. "McKenzie?"

He found a pulse and tried to breathe a little easier as McKenzie's eyes blinked open. What was it about those eyes? "McKenzie. Sweetheart. How badly are you hurt?"

She shook her head and tried to smile through

the pain. "The bastard cut me. His name is Jason Mathews. He—"

"Don't try to talk," he told her. He could hear sirens in the distance. "You're going to be all right. You're safe now."

She closed her eyes as he took her hand. He thought about the first time he'd told her that. It had been a lie. She hadn't been safe. But she would be now, he thought as he looked over at the dead man.

Outside police cars and an ambulance had pulled up. He didn't want to let go of her hand, but he did only long enough to go to the window and direct the EMTs up on the elevator.

As he dropped down onto the bloody floor next to McKenzie again, he realized he was shaking. He thought about what he'd seen the moment he'd cleared the bedroom doorway. McKenzie bound up like that on the floor and that man standing over her, a pair of long-bladed scissors clamped in his hands, the man's beaten face twisted in a grimace—

That was all he remembered until he was on his knees next to McKenzie. He didn't remember pulling the trigger, couldn't even say how many times he'd shot the man.

That thought scared him. He'd been in the P.I. business for ten years. He considered himself a professional. He'd never lost control before.

Suddenly the room was filled with cops and EMTs and a stretcher. He let go of McKenzie's hand and moved back out of the way.

"Is she going to be okay?" he asked as two EMTs went to work on her.

"She's stable. We'll know more once we get her to the hospital."

Hayes wanted desperately to ride in the ambulance with her but one look at the cops and he knew he wasn't going anywhere. "Mind if I call my brother so he can go to the hospital to be with McKenzie until I can get there?"

Chapter Sixteen

McKenzie woke with a start. As her eyes flew open, she saw the woman standing next to her hospital bed. Had she been able to forget yesterday's horror, she might not have recognized the woman at first.

But she hadn't been able to escape Jason Mathews, even filled with anesthesia in the operating room or later in a sedated sleep. He'd followed her into her nightmares.

"Emily Mathews?" She tried to sit up but the woman placed a hand on her shoulder, holding her down on the bed. McKenzie looked up into Jason's wife's face. A pair of dark brown eyes stared back at her.

"I had to see you," the woman said in that small, timid voice McKenzie remembered from the day at the ranchette showing. "Jason's dead, you know."

Dead, but far from forgotten. She tried to sit up again, but she was weak from whatever she'd been given after the surgery. Her side hurt like the devil from where she'd been stabbed. She saw that one of her wrists was bandaged and there was something plastered to her back under her nightgown that burned.

She felt foggy, as if caught between a nightmare and reality. Was this woman even really in her room or was this yet another nightmare?

As she felt the pain and recalled what the madman had done to her, she knew she wasn't dreaming.

"Here, let me do that," Emily said as McKenzie reached for the nurse call button. The woman didn't press it to call a nurse. Instead, she moved it out of her reach.

Fear spiraled through her, making her feel as if she might throw up. Jason was dead but this woman… She tried to sit up again. "What are you—"

The door burst open. McKenzie fell back with such relief that she could no longer hold back the tears. "Hayes." There'd been only one other time she'd been so happy to see him and that had been yesterday. She reminded herself that he'd also saved her the first time they'd met, as he rushed to her bed and took her hand.

"Are you all right?" he asked.

She couldn't speak. Tears rolled down her cheeks as she tried to swallow down the fear that had settled like a dull ache in her chest.

Behind him was a male police officer. "Mrs. Mathews, you shouldn't be in here."

"I had to come," Emily said in her tiniest voice.

"Well, you need to leave now. You're upsetting Ms. Sheldon," the cop said.

"Of course," the woman said, and turned to look at McKenzie. "I'm sorry."

McKenzie thought for a moment that she had misunderstood the woman's intentions. Maybe Emily had only come here to tell her how sorry she was for what her husband had done. But then she looked again in the woman's eyes. There was no compassion. The only emotion burning there was fury.

The woman was sorry, but not for the reasons anyone else in the room thought.

As the policeman led Emily out of the room, she turned to Hayes. "She *knew.* She knew the whole time. Her only regret was that I lived and he died."

Epilogue

"You're going to get sunburned."

McKenzie opened her eyes to look over at Hayes and smiled. "The sun feels so good."

Hayes sat up and reached for the suntan lotion. Since they'd been in Texas, the color had come back into McKenzie's cheeks and she'd gotten a nice tan. She looked healthy, even happy. But he knew she hadn't forgotten her ordeal. Never would. Neither would he.

The scars weren't just on her body, he thought as he rubbed the cool lotion on her back. He'd been surprised when she hadn't wanted to see a plastic surgeon about having the scar on her back removed or the others.

"What would be the point?" she'd said. "For me, it will always be there. Anyway," she'd said, tracing one along his shoulder, "we all have scars."

He remembered each of his scars that he'd gotten growing up with four brothers as well as the ones he'd gotten working as a P.I. Life was dangerous. Sometimes you got lucky and survived it.

"I'm going to be all right, you know," she said when he'd finished applying the lotion.

"I never doubted it."

She sat up to look out at the Gulf of Mexico, her back to him.

"You are the strongest, most determined woman I know."

She smiled at him over her shoulder. She had the most amazing smile. Her hair was even shorter than it had been in Montana. He liked it, but wondered if she missed her long hair. She hadn't known that men like Jason Mathews targeted women with long hair. Women exactly like her. She hadn't known a lot about killers, but she did now.

"I like Texas," she said as she took a deep breath of the gulf air.

He waited, anticipating a "but" before he said, "That's good. You haven't seen much of it yet. It's a big state."

She was watching the waves as she had other days, lying in the sun, wading in the water, seemingly content to spend her days on the beach. The hot sun beat down on the white sand while the surf rolled up only yards from their feet, just as it had all the other days.

Only today, Hayes felt the change in her.

"I've had an offer on the agency," she said after a long moment.

He held his breath, not sure what he wanted her to say. He'd known she couldn't be content spending the rest of her life as a beach bum. That wasn't her. It wasn't him, either. Their lives had been in limbo for weeks now. He'd known she needed time and had been determined to give it to her.

She turned around to face him, sitting cross-legged

on the towel. Her skin was tanned, her high cheekbones pink from the sun, her amazing eyes bright. She looked beautiful. She also looked more confident than he'd seen her in a long time.

"I spoke with your cousin Dana. She wanted to know what our plans are for the wedding."

The sudden shift in subjects threw him off for a moment. "You still want to go to Tag and Lily's wedding?"

"Of course. He's your brother and I adore Lily." She frowned. "You do realize this—" she waved an arm, a motion that encompassed the Galveston beach "—this has been wonderful but only temporary, don't you?"

He nodded. "I've just been waiting for you to get your strength back."

She smiled and placed a cool palm on his bare leg. "What about you?"

"What about me?"

"I know you can afford to spend the rest of your life on this beach if you wanted to, but I don't think that is what you want to do, is it?"

"No, I need to work. Not for the money so much as for the work itself."

She licked her lips, catching her lower lip between her teeth for a moment. He felt a stirring in him, his desire for this woman a constant reminder of how much he loved her and that he hadn't yet told her.

The timing had felt all wrong. He wanted her strong. He wanted that unsinkable McKenzie Sheldon back before he laid that on her.

Now as he looked into her eyes, he saw that she was back.

"There is something I have to tell you," he said as he took both of her hands in his and got his courage up. His parents' marriage had failed. His brother Jackson's, as well. He wasn't sure he ever believed in love ever after, but he damned sure wanted to now.

McKenzie smiled, amusement in her eyes. "Is it that hard to admit?"

He chuckled. "I've been wanting to say it for weeks. I just had to wait until I was sure you were going to be all right."

"I'm all right, Hayes."

"I can see that." He gripped her hands, his gaze locking with hers.

MCKENZIE LOOKED INTO his dark eyes, afraid of what he was going to say. They hadn't talked about the future. She knew he'd made a point of not pushing her. He'd given her time to heal and she loved him for it.

"I love you."

She laughed. "And I love you. I have for a long time."

He let out a relieved breath and pulled her into his arms for a moment. "I want to spend the rest of my life with you. I don't care where it is as long as we're together."

"Are you saying you would go back to Montana with me?"

"If that is what you want. I could open a private-investigation business in Bozeman or even in the canyon. Dana was telling me about a ranch near hers that was going on the market. I would need a good real-estate agent to handle things."

She couldn't believe what he was saying. "After staying at the Cardwell Ranch, I'm spoiled to live anywhere but the canyon. Could we really do this?"

"Only if you agree to marry me." He looked into her eyes again. "But be sure. This is a no-holds-barred offer till death do us part with kids and dogs and horses and barbecues behind the house."

She laughed as she threw herself back into his arms, knocking them to the sand. "Yes," she said as she looked down into his handsome face. "Yes to all of it."

"And I haven't even made you any Texas Boys Barbecue yet." He flipped her over so he was on top. "Woman, you are in for a treat."

She sobered as she looked up at him. "You've saved my life in so many ways," she said as she touched his cheek. "Do you think it was fate that night that we met?"

"I don't know. But I think I knew the moment I first looked into your eyes that you were the only woman who could get this Texas boy out of Texas."

He kissed her with a promise of good things to come as the surf rolled up to their feet and Montana called.

* * * * *

COMING NEXT MONTH FROM

HARLEQUIN®

INTRIGUE®

Available June 17, 2014

#1503 WEDDING AT CARDWELL RANCH

Cardwell Cousins • by B.J. Daniels

Someone is hell-bent on making Allie Taylor think she's losing her mind. Allie's past has stalked her to Cardwell Ranch, and not even Jackson Cardwell may be able to save her from a killer with a chilling agenda.

#1504 HARD RIDE TO DRY GULCH

Big "D" Dads: The Daltons • by Joanna Wayne

Faith Ashburn turns to sexy detective Travis Dalton to find and save her missing son. In the process, will Travis lose his heart and find a family?

#1505 UNDERCOVER WARRIOR

Copper Canyon • by Aimée Thurlo

Was Agent Kyle Goodluck's last undercover assignment too close to home for comfort? Now Kyle's only hope to prevent an attack that would rock the entire nation is the mysterious woman he's just rescued from terrorists, Erin Barrett.

#1506 EXPLOSIVE ENGAGEMENT

Shotgun Weddings • by Lisa Childs

Stacy Kozminski and Logan Payne must fake an engagement to survive. But with someone trying to kill them with bullets and bombs, they may never make it to the altar.

#1507 STRANDED

The Rescuers • by Alice Sharpe

When detective Alex Foster returns from the dead, he wants two things: his estranged, pregnant wife, Jessica, to love him, and to capture the man who wants them both dead....

#1508 SANCTUARY IN CHEF VOLEUR

The Delancey Dynasty • by Mallory Kane

Hannah Martin flees to New Orleans looking for help from PI Mack Griffin. It doesn't take him long to appreciate Hannah's courage and resourcefulness, or to realize that he may end up needing protection, too—from his feelings for her.

SPECIAL EXCERPT FROM

HARLEQUIN

INTRIGUE

Read on for a sneak peek of
WEDDING AT CARDWELL RANCH
by New York Times *bestselling author*

B.J. Daniels

Part of the ***CARDWELL COUSINS*** *series.*

In Montana for his brother's nuptials, Jackson Cardwell isn't looking to be anybody's hero. But the Texas single father knows a beautiful lady in distress when he meets her.

"I'm afraid to ask what you just said to your horse," Jackson joked as he moved closer. Her horse had wandered over to some tall grass away from the others.

"Just thanking him for not bucking me off," she admitted shyly.

"Probably a good idea, but your horse is a she. A mare."

"Oh, hopefully she wasn't insulted." Allie actually smiled. The afternoon sun lit her face along with the smile.

He felt his heart do a loop-de-loop. He tried to rein it back in as he looked into her eyes. That tantalizing green was deep and dark, inviting, and yet he knew a man could drown in those eyes.

Suddenly, Allie's horse shied. In the next second it took off as if it had been shot from a cannon. To her credit, she hadn't let go of her reins, but she grabbed the saddle horn and let out a cry as the mare raced out of the meadow headed for the road.

Jackson spurred his horse and raced after her. He could hear the startled cries of the others behind him. He'd been riding since he was a boy, so he knew how to handle his horse. But Allie, he could see, was having trouble staying in the saddle with her horse at a full gallop.

He pushed his horse harder and managed to catch her, riding alongside until he could reach over and grab her reins. The horses lunged along for a moment. Next to him Allie started to fall. He grabbed for her, pulling her from her saddle and into his arms as he released her reins and brought his own horse up short.

Allie slid down his horse to the ground. He dismounted and dropped beside her. "Are you all right?"

"I think so. What happened?"

He didn't know. One minute her horse was munching on grass, the next it had taken off like a shot.

Allie had no idea why the horse had reacted like that. She hated that she was the one who'd upset everyone.

"Are you sure you didn't spur your horse?" Natalie asked, still upset.

"She isn't wearing spurs," Ford pointed out.

"Maybe a bee stung your horse," Natalie suggested.

Dana felt bad. "I wanted your first horseback-riding experience to be a pleasant one," she lamented.

"It was. It is," Allie reassured her, although in truth, she wasn't looking forward to getting back on the horse. But she knew she had to for Natalie's sake. The kids had been scared enough as it was.

Dana had spread out the lunch on a large blanket with the kids all helping when Jackson rode up, trailing her horse. The mare looked calm now, but Allie wasn't sure she would ever trust it again.

Jackson met her gaze as he dismounted. Dana was already on her feet, heading for him. Allie left the kids to join them.

"What is it?" Dana asked, keeping her voice down.

Jackson looked to Allie as if he didn't want to say in front of her.

"Did I do something to the horse to make her do that?" she asked, fearing that she had.

His expression softened as he shook his head. "You didn't do *anything*." He looked at Dana. "Someone shot the mare."

Someone is hell-bent on making Allie Taylor think she's losing her mind. Jackson's determined to unmask the perp. Can he guard the widowed wedding planner and her little girl from a killer with a chilling agenda?